The Strange Accounts of Germantown

and Other Peculiar Phenomena

Front cover image by Khaighnen White
Book design by Khaighnen White

Edited by Paige Lawson

ISBN: 9798356014369

All inquiries may be directed to kaysynclaire@gmail.com

Imprint: Independently published
Mineral Spring Publishing
www.kaysynclaire.squarespace.com

For lovers of all things wholesome and creepy.

And also to our mother, who bestowed upon us the love of writing.

To whom this book is gift'd,
Ye must place no blame
Greet one with a brotherly kiss
And know keepers ne'er regain

Do not delay, do not elude
Ye must find the time
These eight stories ye must conclude
Lest ye make it nine

Contents

i. bryan

I was new to Philadelphia. I moved into the
Germantown neighborhood about six months ago from New
York where I'd been alone for quite some time. I had friends, of
course, but never found someone special who I felt I could
settle down with. With the astronomical rent increases, my best
friend and I growing apart due to a nasty argument, and an
almost non-existent love life, deciding to leave was easy.

Kayla, my younger half-sister, resided in Philadelphia,
living in the house our mother left us when she died seven years
ago. It was the ultimate factor in choosing to come to the city
of not-so-brotherly love.

At thirty-one, I figured I should make an attempt to
cultivate a relationship with the only family I had left. The
transition was easy enough since I worked remotely most of the
time. Occasionally, I'd need to visit New York for projects that

required a hands-on approach. Since Septa runs almost continuously, getting back to New York was no issue.

Kayla was a twenty-seven-year-old artsy, high-energy, people person. She worked full-time as a waitress for some fancy restaurant in Center City and sometimes brought home more in tips than I did in a single paycheck. In her spare time she would sign up to work on various local plays and thus, was known by many. People loved her - gravitated towards her - and it'd been like that all our lives.

We had different fathers. My dad left when I was young, and my stepdad, David, took his place. Although I'm white and he was black, no one could tell me he wasn't my father. He took me to Phillies games, attended my school conferences, and even participated in carpooling for my sports meets.

My mom had Kayla four years later, and though I have no proof, I felt the relationship between David and I changed for the worse. Whether I meant to or not, I blamed Kayla, and years later, we only spoke on holidays or when there was a problem, like our mom's unexpected passing.

I remembered how the conversation transpired when I told her I was considering a permanent move to Philly. I wanted to gauge her reaction before requesting to move in with her. When I was twenty-four, my mother left the house to both of us, but I wanted nothing to do with it.

When I finally mustered enough courage to call her this past April, she'd been quiet on the other end of the phone. I had just spilled my guts to her, apologizing for leaving her all this time and that I regretted leaving when she needed me the most.

I held my breath. She was silent. She had been at work when I called. I heard the cacophony of dishes clanging, orders being yelled out, and the random conversations of patrons. My stomach churned, and my heart raced waiting for a response.

She sighed. "The utilities will need to be split. Any work needed on the house will be our shared responsibility. I don't always cook dinner, but when I do, you're welcome to it." I'm unsure if she could tell, but I began crying. My voice trembled, barely above a whisper, "Thank you," and she hung up.

The week I moved in, Kayla decided to take a trip. Her friends invited her to the Poconos for a girls only retreat. We saw each other for a brief moment before she rushed out. She gave me a deflated hug and a quick rundown on where to find things before darting out the door.

"Sorry, Bryan!" she yelled as she shouldered her duffel bag. "I'm gonna miss the train. I gotta go!"

I followed her out the front door to watch her jog down the street. I saw her suddenly stop and pull something from her duffel bag. She bent down in the street near the corner, looking over her shoulder just before sprinting towards the train station.

"Kayla, you are so weird," I mumbled with a chuckle.

When I stepped back inside, I took in my childhood home. Kayla had gotten some work done to the house, but she kept all our mom's favorite family photos on the wall. The layout was different, more modern and intentionally placed. The gallery was illuminated by tastefully chosen sconce lighting.

I stopped at a photo of me sitting on a couch, my legs too short to reach the floor. I was holding Kayla, who was bundled tightly in the receiving blanket she left the hospital in. My face beamed with pride. Our mom sat beside us, one hand securing her newest precious babe and one on me. She was flashing a mother's smile; proud, exhausted, and happy.

Looking around the house again, the furniture was laid out differently too, but my childhood home was mostly how I remembered it. There was a scent of vanilla, cinnamon, and earthy wood. Years ago, two white built-in pillars separated the living and dining rooms, but they'd been replaced with large built-in bookshelves. Maybe that's where the woodsy scent was coming from.

I looked over the new bookshelves and ran my finger over numerous spines, old and new, big and small, until my finger rested on a frayed, loose-bound book. I gingerly pulled at the top, just enough to get a peek at the title. I was surprised when I didn't see one. Curiosity getting the best of me, I pulled it completely out and turned to the first page.

Resting inside was an old, yellowing newspaper clipping. I read the title.

Crash on Lincoln Drive, 23rd Victim This Year.

I looked at the photo of the wreckage, searching for some suggestion that this was David. When I looked at the date of publication, it immediately sent chills up my spine- Kayla's ninth birthday- the day her dad died.

It was tragic. David had forgotten to pick me up from baseball practice in the chaos of prepping for her birthday party. My coach waited for me as I cried to my mom on the phone that I'd been forgotten.

Years later, my mom told me what had happened that night. When David finally got home from the store, bags in hand, my mom yelled at him for forgetting me. She was on her way out the door when David apologized and took the keys. He told her, "It's okay, Lynne. I'll pick up our son."

He never made it to me, though. He died on Lincoln Drive, or *Dead Man's Gulch*, an oft-traveled, winding, dangerous road that claimed the lives of many.

The night that David died, someone crossed the median and hit him head-on. He skirted off the road, landing upside down in the creek. They said he died on impact.

Soon after, my mom fell into depression, never forgiving herself for the angry words she spewed towards the man she loved and letting him go instead. And I never forgave myself either. I knew he'd never purposely forget me.

Kayla went through her birthday gifts a few weeks later, and at the sight of her opening them, I went to my room. I couldn't bear it.

I jumped at the sound of a knock on my door. It was a tearful Kayla holding a gift bag, and my mom stifling back her sobs. Kayla handed the bag to me.

Confused, I grabbed it and peered inside. Moving the tissue paper around, I finally laid eyes on a baseball helmet and a brand-new glove. David was late picking me up because while getting presents for Kayla, he'd wanted to get me something, too.

Somewhere in my young mind, anger, grief, sadness, and confusion led me to Kayla. I believed if she hadn't begged for the birthday party, our dad would still be here.

Of course, with maturing, I understood my thinking was flawed, but it was too late. Our relationship was already estranged. My mom tried her hardest to get us back together, but sadly, even her death couldn't do it. And the guilt had been eating away at me ever since, leading me to numerous therapists, antidepressants, and benzodiazepine trials.

I thumbed to the next page of the loosely bound book and saw a flattened bundle of charred leaves. They were snuggly tied with a string. For some reason, I lifted the book to my nose to inhale the plant's scent. The odor made me dizzy, and I had to grab onto the bookshelf for balance.

"What the hell, Kayla?" I shook my head and slapped the book closed, placing it back where I found it.

The movers were coming the next day with my things, and I needed to get some sleep. I walked up to my old bedroom. It hadn't really been disturbed. There were some storage boxes stacked in the corner. Some of my things were gone, but the bed was made for me.

That was nice of Kayla, I thought, as I peeled back the blankets. I heard a faint meow and was surprised to see Mia, our old tabby, crawl from underneath the bed. I scratched behind her ears, and she allowed me. We didn't always get along, but I was genuinely happy to see her. She jumped up to sit at the slightly cracked window and looked out. It was going to rain which almost always helped me nap. I unpacked a few things from my bookbag, took my meds, and drifted asleep.

—

I sat on the edge of my bed, electricity flowing from head to toe. My heart was pounding hard. I'd heard sounds coming from outside.

I grabbed the cup of room-temperature water sitting on my nightstand and forced myself to guzzle it down. I attempted to slow my heart rate and anxiety level by doing some deep breathing, taught to me by my therapist. It allowed me to finally take stock of my bedroom.

I jumped at the projection of what appeared to be a tall, thin figure wearing a hat looming across my wall, but quickly realized the boxes were to blame. Why was I so damn jumpy? I got up and rearranged them so that their shadow no longer resembled a man standing in my room. I stared at my door, slightly ajar, the dim light from the hallway trickling in and became acutely aware of my solitude.

The house was still, not a sound heard except the rotating fan in the corner of my room. I clicked it off and went back to bed to listen for the sound that woke me up.

After stewing in silence, I made a mental note to call Dr. Andrews in the morning about this new anti-anxiety med. It was disturbing my sleep and sanity.

I whipped the blankets back over my legs, pissed for being woken up for no obvious reason when... there it was. The sound again. It was faint, but I knew I wasn't mistaken.

It was the soft whinny of horses.

It was coming from outside. My heart thumped as I stood at the window closest to my bed. I hid by standing left of the window frame and peeled the curtain back enough to see out.

Across the street, under the soft, orange glow of a streetlamp, a dark silhouette crouched down on the sidewalk. A light fog blanketed the cobblestone street, but I could see that his attention focused downward as if searching for something he'd dropped. A tall black hat sat atop his head, but I couldn't quite make out the details of his face.

He reached into the street and retrieved what looked to be a pocket watch on a long gold chain that flickered in the dim light. Then I heard the faint clinking of coins hitting the ground.

As he stood erect, my throat dried up. His willow, thin frame seamlessly unfolded, revealing a man inexplicably tall. The brim of his hat obscured his face.

He looked at his watch, then down Germantown Avenue when he saw what he'd been waiting for.

An old-style carriage with no coachman was being pulled by two horses, the sound of their hooves echoing against the centuries old cobblestone. The carriage slowed to a stop in front of the man.

He placed one gloved hand on the carriage to help himself inside, but he was too tall. He began to contort his body. His shoulders jerked and twitched, his head spasming in quick fitful movements. It set off a deep panic inside me like nothing I'd ever known.

I realized he was shrinking himself to fit inside the carriage. I felt sick to my stomach. I held the windowsill to keep from falling over when he abruptly stopped his transmutation and snapped his head towards the other side of the street. My street.

His attention locked on the window beside me. When he looked up, I saw his two tiny, yellow eyes. He hissed loudly, his mouth opened, growing larger and larger.

I cursed and jumped back, tripping over a box and landing halfway on the bed. My head whipped towards the window that captured his attention to see Mia sitting in the open window gazing outside.

The sound of my heartbeat in my ears, and my body trembling with fear only heightened my anxiety. Did it see me? What the hell was that thing?

I peeked through the glass pane.

Nothing was there.

I sat on the bed, closed my eyes, and gripped my bed sheets, feeling lightheaded; that's when I realized I'd been holding my breath. According to the clock, I'd been up for an hour. Impossible. I looked at the orange pill bottle on my nightstand in disgust. *Great. Now I'm hallucinating*, I thought.

I pulled the blankets over my legs again. I must've been hallucinating, but I needed to know if I imagined an eight-foot man outside or not.

I peeled back the curtain one last time and saw an empty street corner. I exhaled a deep breath and looked over at Mia who was staring at me. She jumped down with a thud and sauntered out, tail swishing in the air.

—

I woke up with a start and thought about how unsettling my first night home was. Thankfully, I heeded a friend's advice and took the week off from work to get settled. It made an easier transition without the pressure of work breathing down my neck. I had lots of boring things to do and needed to get started. Speaking with Dr. Andrews was first. I left a message with the nurse about the side effects of my current meds and my need for a change. With that first order of business done, I hopped up to start my day.

Living in New York, I didn't need a car and was very accustomed to walking. That was something I also got to enjoy about Germantown. I could walk anywhere I needed.

Red Sun Cafe was near enough to walk so I picked up my order and was on my way home within thirty minutes. As I walked home, I took in how much the neighborhood had changed. Germantown High School closed down in 2013. Something about money, but I heard rumors that the place was haunted. Now, it was in the process of being renovated into apartments. On Germantown Avenue, there were shops, homes, and markets I'd never seen before. It was a lot different than I remembered, and it'd only been seven years since I'd left.

When I put my key in the door, I looked up and noticed a small camera to the left of the porch light. I hadn't seen it the other day. The camera wasn't pointed at the front door; it was directed outward toward the corner of Germantown and Tulpehocken streets. Without a thought, I walked over to where I saw the man last night. I didn't know what I expected to find. I scanned the sidewalk where I saw the man recover his pocket watch, and a rush of blood shot to my head as I bent down to pick up three silver coins.

They were coins unlike any that I'd ever seen before. They were embossed with filigree and the words *one dime* were written in the middle. I stared at them for a few seconds before putting them in my pocket. I jogged back to the house. I didn't have access to the security camera, but I made a mental note to ask Kayla about it.

I spent the day orchestrating movers, making phone calls, cleaning, and by sundown, I was finally all moved in. I ordered some Chinese food and scoured Netflix for something good to watch. I decided on a documentary but after a few minutes, I opened my laptop to search for information on the mysterious coins.

A quick Google search revealed that they were early 19th-century coins, but they weren't really worth anything. I felt a bit bummed that the coins were useless so I tossed them in a handmade catch-all on Kayla's new bookshelf. When I did, a tiny red blinking light caught my eye. Tucked up in the corner of the living room, above the front door, was a small black camera. Seeing a second camera prompted me to review the text thread with Kayla to see if I'd missed her telling me about the security system. I hadn't.

I was starting to feel slightly bothered, maybe even a bit paranoid. The hair on my arms stood on end. Thinking about it, I hadn't heard from Kayla since moving in.

Didn't she want to ensure everything went well here? But I stopped myself. We didn't have the best sibling relationship *and* she was enjoying time with friends. Not getting a text wasn't all that peculiar. I stared at the blinking red light, wondering if Kayla had access to the camera while she was away. I wondered if she could see me now. If she was watching me.

Mia scurried across the floor between my legs and broke me from my trance.

I cleaned up my takeout from the living room and brought my dirty dishes to the kitchen. I opened the newly installed dishwasher and it only made me wonder, "How the hell is she affording all of this?"

After stacking the dishes, I saw yet another shiny black camera resting in the farthest corner of the kitchen and now I really couldn't shake the feeling of being watched. Why would Kayla want to watch me? Did she not trust me?

I went back to the living room to finish my beer, but my attention went back to Kayla's impressive bookshelf. I ogled her collection again, looking over the coins in the catch-all before looking at more books. I didn't know Kayla to be so well-read.

I saw the loosely bound, frayed book again and skipped over it. Beside it was a book with extremely thick text on a gold embossed label.

"*The Kin's Text*, huh?" I flipped through the hardback and there were hand-drawn illustrations, some handwritten passages, some typed text. Some of the passages were in languages I had never seen before which wasn't saying much. I wasn't a linguist by any stretch of the imagination.

I found a dog-eared page and carefully opened it. It was historical information about Philadelphia, Germantown specifically. There were multiple depictions of old Germantown - the streets, the trolleys, and in very early times, horse-drawn carriages.

I stopped and studied an illustration of our very own street. Next to a horse-drawn carriage was a picture of a thin man dressed in all black. He was tall, wore a top hat, and hanging from his trousers was a pocket watch equipped with a thin chain.

My eyes repeatedly blinked as if trying to clear the image from my mind when my phone rang, startling me. It was Kayla.

I answered dumbly. "Uh, hey."

There was a pause at the end of her line, but she finally spoke. "Yeah, um, are you okay? I'm just, uh, checking on you."

I looked up at the camera before answering. "Yeah, I'm just sitting here watching a documentary. Thanks for asking. How's your trip-"

"Oh okay. That's good. Also, just to let you know, since you're having movers come in and out of the house, I collect weird things. It's just what I'm into, and I'd rather they leave my things as they are. Untouched."

Silence.

"Yeah, Kayla, no problem. I'm all moved in. I made sure they didn't touch your stuff-"

"I don't want you touching them either, Bryan," she snapped, but then she fell silent before speaking again. "Did you have a pretty uneventful day?" she asked slowly, trying to find the safest words to say. I didn't know how to answer.

"Well, I tried that coffee shop, Red Sun. I got lots of errands done," I paused, thinking about my next sentence. If she were watching me, she'd know about the coins.

"I actually found some old-style coins today."

She fell silent again then she exhaled. "Hm, that's cool," she said, dragging the *-oo*. "You should put them back, Bryan. The coins. Just put them back where you got them." And just like that, she ended the call.

I looked up at the camera then back to the coins in the raggedy catch-all. I didn't know what the hell Kayla was into, but I preferred to stay out of it. Kayla had access to the cameras in the house and thus, had seen exactly how the move went and knew that I went through her book collection. She felt the need to warn me that I shouldn't touch her things. Fine.

The cryptic warning to toss century-old coins back into the street? Maybe I could refer her to my doctor.

It was a long day so I decided to shower and head to bed early. Subconsciously, I was nervous about having a repeat of the first night.

When I got dressed for bed, I glanced out the window at the corner of Germantown and Tulpehocken. It was only half past nine, so cars still crawled up and down the street. It gave me temporary comfort that everything was as it always had been. But seeing the nauseating glow of the orange streetlights triggered last night's nightmare so I closed and locked both windows. I played some white noise to help me get comfortable enough to drift off to sleep.

—

My eyes popped open and I stared at the ceiling. I dreaded looking at the alarm clock.

"Please be morning," I pleaded, slowly turning my head towards the green glow of the clock. My prayers were not answered. It was 3:20 in the morning. I thought hard about what caused me to wake up. The orange pill bottle was absent from my bedside table, a glass of water in its place. I remembered putting it away so I didn't take any meds before bed.

My bedroom door was closed, and the soft glow of the hallway lamp illuminated a strip of light across the hardwood floor. Mia was scratching to get out. She was the culprit.

"Mia..." I grumbled, but I breathed a sigh of relief.

I got up to let her out when suddenly a slender shadow quickly, but temporarily, blocked the section of light spilling under my door.

I stopped in my tracks. Mia's cries grew louder, her paws digging at the bottom of the door. My heart beat so hard against my chest, it felt like it was pushing me forward.

I grabbed Mia and backed away from the door. I bumped against the window and glanced out, praying that there was nothing but parked cars outside. Slowly pulling back the curtains, my eyes darted across the street to the empty corner of Germantown and Tulpehocken and back.

My shoulders relaxed slightly until I looked down. I shook my head, witnessing two horses and an old black carriage stopped in front of the house. The horses swayed left to right, and they whinnied, and stomped impatiently.

"No, no." I snapped my head towards the bedroom door when I saw the light completely blocked this time. The hardwood floor creaked on the other side of my door.

The door handle turned slowly from left to right, right to left. In my paranoia last night, I had locked my bedroom door. I grabbed the chair from my desk and forced it under the doorknob. The handle stopped moving.

I slowly backed away from the door again when a bang sounded on the door, and Mia and I both jumped.

I dove into my bed to get my phone and dialed Kayla's number. "Come on Kayla, come on, pick up," I whispered, but the call went to voicemail.

More knocks on the door, this time harder, angrier. I yelped and crouched at the head of my bed. Mia had run underneath, meowing and hissing incessantly.

The knocks came quicker, pounding with so much force that I was sure it would break down any moment.

Then suddenly it stopped. The floor creaked again, and I crawled to the foot of bed, as if getting off would assure my doom. I turned on my phone's flashlight and pointed it at the bottom of the door.

A gloved hand, long and slender, emerged from beneath it. It moved back and forth frantically, trying to grab a hold of something.

The horses clomped against the cobblestone outside in a frenzy, Mia's cries grew louder and all the sounds seemed to blend into one. I felt faint.

"Shit!" Someone cried outside, and I knelt on my bed to look out the window. It was Kayla. She was running toward the corner of Germantown and Tulpehocken, but stopped when she dropped something. I heard the clinking of coins falling on the sidewalk.

At the sound, the hand underneath my door quickly retracted.

I looked out the window and Kayla was on the corner now, tossing the coins into the street. Back where I had found them. I saw her shoulders move as she took a deep breath and looked up into my window.

The horses and the old carriage faded away as though they'd never been there.

Mia sauntered back out from beneath the bed with a soft meow. I stayed still, I didn't want to get up, but then I heard the front door open and slam downstairs.

"Kayla?" I called as I came down.

She was in the kitchen, only the stove light was on, but she was rifling through the cabinets to get out a pan. I watched her turn on the stove and get bacon from the refrigerator.

"Hey, Bryan," she said over her shoulder as she started frying the bacon. "You want eggs and bacon?"

"Um, no. What the hell, Kayla?"

She finally turned to face me with a knowing smile on her face. "Relax. We're safe now. Have a seat and I'll tell you everything."

We sat in the dining room, and I watched Kayla silently as she poured a glass of orange juice. She set a plate of bacon and eggs before me and sat down. The clock above the archway that led into the kitchen said it was five in the morning. It didn't feel like all of that lasted almost two hours. In any case, I wasn't hungry. But apparently Kayla was. She didn't wait to tear into her food.

"God, I was so hungry." She shook her head in bliss, but then paused when she saw my bewildered face. "What?"

"What the hell happened?" I shouted.

"Oh, right. Okay, sorry." She wiped her mouth with a napkin. "A few weeks ago, I was on my way to work when I saw something in the street. On the corner," she said motioning towards the front door.

"It was an old-timey watch. It looked kind of valuable so I took it. I did some research and the damn thing was worth fifty thousand dollars!"

I nodded for her to continue.

"So," she continued. "I have, you know, high profile clientele at the restaurant. I told one of my regulars about it, and he wanted to buy it for a hundred thousand. I was so excited, I didn't think about it. I just took the money. I spent a lot of it on the house, fixing things up."

She took a bite of bacon and shook her head. "I should have known better, though, because the day after I sold it, I heard horses and shit outside. That tall thing was following me everywhere. Inside the house, outside, on the train, at work. I was going crazy. I didn't know what to do. The guy I sold it to never came back to the restaurant.

"I tried everything to protect myself. I put in a security system, but that thing could still get in the house without tripping the alarm. I told my coworker about it, and he suggested putting the watch back where I found it.

"So with his help, we found where the buyer lived and kind of stole it back." She shrugged her shoulders as she took a sip of orange juice. "I returned the watch where I found it... actually, the day you moved in. I went on my trip with my friends, and I didn't see that thing following me anymore. But when you said you found the coins, I got worried."

She pointed to the camera in the corner of the living room. "I saw where you put them and noticed you didn't listen to me. So, I came home to do it and saved your sorry ass."

My face felt hot and I rubbed the back of my neck. "Yeah, thanks for that."

"No problem. Ketchup?" she asked, with a mouth full of eggs.

It amazed me how Kayla could just pick herself back up like life was normal. I didn't deserve her coming back to save me even when I didn't listen to her and thought she was a little crazy.

We sat there for hours and talked until the sun rose. I apologized again for leaving her side. We both cried when she accepted the apology.

I'm more than relieved to say that neither of us have seen or heard any horses, or strange men in top hats.

ii. kiya

I can barely keep my eyes open. I pour creamer into the coffee until it forms a rippled leaf. My hand knocks over a stack of coffee lids when I try to grab one and Fran chuckles.

"Tired?" she asks. She brushes past me to get a tray of pastries from the oven.

I slide the coffee to the edge of the counter. "Hank?" I call and a young man walks up, wearing black hipster glasses and suspenders. He smiles at me, and I wait until he's gone before turning to Fran. "I had to pull another all-nighter. I'm falling behind in Chem."

"He was cute." Fran nods towards the guy with the suspenders. He's standing by the shop's front door, holding the coffee lid in his teeth as he tries to snap a picture of my subpar latte art.

I groan. "Please, I'd rather fail Chem."

"He's too eccentric for you?"

"Eccentric?" I nearly laugh. "No, besides, I have other things to worry about." I don't mean to yawn, but Fran chuckles again.

"Okay, I get it. You're a tired college student." She rolls her eyes. "I'm just saying, it wouldn't hurt to meet someone." She leans on the counter. Her long locs are tied back under a paisley bandana, and her apron is smudged with coffee stains. She has wrinkles around her eyes because Fran likes to laugh. A lot.

She owns the Red Sun Cafe and barely hesitated when I asked for a job. I was a struggling college student with no experience. I had never worked a day in my life, but she didn't mind as long as I could work now. I thought she'd only care about my job performance, like make sure I come in on time and don't mess up orders. But unfortunately, I'm a little *too* good, because she has nothing to comment on *except* my social life. She means well, but goodness, she can really hound someone until they cave in.

"You know, there's more to life than other people," I say.

She moves out of the way as I wipe down the counters. She has a pensive look on her face. "If you think that, you'll lead a very sad life."

"I'll be fine," I say as the cafe door dings.

"Speaking of fine!" Fran's smile takes up half of her face, and she waves her arm. "Hey boo!"

It's the mailman and Fran's crush of the month. He's stocky, with starter locs, and slinging a frayed blue bag over his shoulder. He grins at Fran. "Got mail for Francheska Howard."

"That's me." Fran leans over the counter and bats her lashes.

I chuckle and thankfully, more customers come in so I don't have to see this gushy display. It's not that I don't like love; it's just... Well, I've never had it.

Before long, the lunch rush comes so all thoughts of my crippling love life vanish. Fran has to say goodbye to her mailman. She still finds a way through the bustle to tell me she has a date with him.

"All you have to do is ask, Kiya," she says and then in the next breath calls out an order for an iced pumpkin coffee.

I grind my teeth and push through my shift. Normally, I'd ignore Fran's *suggestions* about finding someone, but the words, *'you'll lead a sad life'* is all I can think about.

My shift soon ends, and I take care of one last customer. He's a guy with broad shoulders. He has stubble on his face, but it's still groomed. He's wearing black sunglasses despite it getting later in the day.

"Medium black," he says. He takes off his glasses and stares into my eyes. It's intimidating, so I have to look away. "Hendrix fan?"

The question takes me off guard and he's smiling, looking at my shirt.

I answer with a chuckle. "Yeah, actually. Are you?"

"Of course." He opens his jacket to reveal a similar Jimi Hendrix shirt with different neon colors. "You have great taste."

"Thanks, you, too." I don't know why my voice goes up an octave, but it's enough for Fran to take notice. I can feel her eyes burning the side of my face as she rolls dough.

I ignore her. "Can I have a name for the coffee?"

"Benjamin." He winks as he puts his sunglasses on top of his head, and I can't explain what that simple move does to my stomach. I scribble his name on the side of the cup.

"Okay, I'll have it ready soon."

Fran comes to my side once I hide behind the french press and she wiggles her brows.

"Do it."

"Do what?"

"Ask him out."

"I will not," I laugh. My cheeks feel hot.

"Well, okay. That may be too advanced for you. But he's been here before. I saw him checking you out, but I didn't want to say anything. So, here-" she hands me a pen, "write your number on his cup."

I brush her hand away. "You're crazy."

I finish his order, but my mind is spinning. When I glance over the counter, he's reading a book as he patiently waits. Without his direct eye contact, I feel like I can finally see him. He bites his nail as he scans the page. He's wearing dark jeans and a leather jacket over his Hendrix shirt. Keys rest from his waist with little gold guitar charms. Does he play guitar?

He doesn't *actively* disgust me. Not like some of the guys I go to school with. And besides, who says that we have to date. We could... we could talk about Jimi Hendrix or books... and now, I'm picturing a whole life with this man.

I place the lid on the coffee cup. While Fran is busy with another customer, I write my number on the side.

"Benjamin," I call and he looks right up. I swallow. "Your coffee, Benjamin."

He grins again and I don't remember him having dimples. He takes the coffee. "Please, call me Ben."

"Great, and maybe *you* can call *me*." My eyes shift to the coffee and I swear, I have an out-of-body experience. Because *where* did that line come from? Did I sound stupid? Shoot, does he have a girlfriend already? Why did I ever listen to Fran?

But then Ben looks at the cup and chuckles. "Oh. Oh, I think I will. Your name?"

My hands are sweaty. "Kiya."

He reaches to shake my hand, and a bandage is covering his wrist. I don't want to stare so I shake his hand quickly.

"Pleasure to meet you, Kiya."

And just like that, he's out of the cafe.

—

I get out of the shower later that night, and I twist my damp hair. My apartment is a studio, dimly lit courtesy of the lamp near my tv. My chemistry notes are sprawled before me on the couch, and I'm muttering formulas.

Rain trickles down my window. I get up to close the blinds, but I pause. It's dark outside. The steeple from the big church across the street rests against the moonlit sky.

And across the street, I see something strange. Two red dots hover in the darkness. I think I see the outline of a figure.

A car drives by and the headlights briefly cover the street. There's nothing there, but the red dots hover for a second before disappearing.

"Okay, I'm just gonna..." I close the blinds and go back to my chem notes. I'm just minding my Black business. I didn't see anything.

Before I can get deep into studying, my phone rings. "Hello?"

"Hi. Is this Kiya?" The voice is smooth.

I sit up straighter on the couch. "Benjamin?"

"Ben," he corrects with a smile in his voice. "No need to be so formal."

"Ben." I stand on my feet because I don't know what else to do with my body. "Thanks for calling."

"It's my pleasure."

I peek through the blinds at the rain falling harshly now. A strike of lightning crosses the sky. "It's pouring out."

Thunder booms from his end on the call. "Yeah, I like it though. It soothes me."

"Me, too, actually." I close the blinds and walk aimlessly around my apartment.

It's so strange talking to Ben. He's calm. When I speak, he stops and listens. It feels like he weighs his words before he speaks them. The conversation is strangely refreshing and as I settle back onto the couch thirty minutes later, I feel my eyelids getting heavy.

He offers to meet on Kelly Drive tomorrow evening for a walk and I'm a little embarrassed at how fast I agree.

"I'll see you tomorrow, Kiya."

"I'll see you tomorrow, Ben."

I never make it to my bed. My notes will be there for me in the morning.

—

Kelly Drive is beautiful this time of year. The trees have shed their pink flowers from the summer and now yellow, orange, and red leaves blow in the wind. White string lights are woven into the trees spaced down the walkway. It isn't too late in the evening, so kids are still playing near the water as their parents watch from the grass, lying on top of blankets.

Class couldn't let out fast enough. I rushed from school to come down here to meet Ben. And to be honest, I'm not really excited. I'm *nervous as hell*. I've never done this before. Is this normal? Do girls get jittery when asked on a date? Is this even a date? He never said it was.

I walk amongst the trees where Ben said to meet. I'm a little early. My anxiety wouldn't let me arrive just in time. I had to scope the land and see the place for myself first, even though I've been to Kelly Drive a thousand times.

A few minutes later, Ben strides down the path carrying a small bouquet of petunias. He's still wearing those sunglasses, but I can feel his intense stare burning behind them. He grins wide when he sees me.

"Hey, these are for you." He hands me the flowers. "I don't know if these are your favorite, but we talked about petunias last night."

My face feels hot. "Thank you. No, this is thoughtful. Thank you." I'm bumbling like an idiot. "God, I'm sorry, I didn't bring anything for you."

He laughs. "It's okay, Kiya. Don't worry." He extends his elbow, and I take it tentatively. "Shall we?"

I have no idea what universe I've accidentally stumbled into. We stroll through the illuminated trees as the sun sets over the river. He actually makes me laugh, and I feel myself, as time wears on, loosening my shoulders and my jaw.

It gets dark and we decide to sit beneath a tree, but not before he takes off his leather jacket and fans it on the ground. I glance at his shirt and smile. "More Hendrix?"

"Always more Hendrix." He laughs as he settles beside me. My attention falls on the bandage still wrapped over his wrist. I try not to notice it again, but he catches on. "Oh." He flexes his hand and stares at it.

"Can I ask what happened?"

Ben shrugs. "It's a long story...kinda. Got into some trouble a few nights ago on Halloween."

I raise my brows. "Trouble?"

"Yeah." His mouth stretches into a smile. "But don't worry, you should see the other guy."

"So it was a fight."

He nods. "Yeah, in a way."

"Are you a troublemaker?" I say, trying to sound flirtatious, but I'm still very curious about the answer.

Ben sits back and looks at me head-on. His gaze suddenly makes me feel like I'm under a spotlight. "Does that frighten you?"

My smile falters. "Maybe."

He reaches out for my hand, and I let him have it. "I went out on Halloween with some friends. I went home early and on the train coming back, some guy attacked me. He had a knife and cut me up pretty bad. I had to get a few stitches. That's all." He closed his fingers around my hand. "I'm not dangerous. I promise."

My hand tightens in his grip. I'm not sure if it's the lights, or the river, or just... him, but I lean in and give him a chaste kiss. It's experimental and soft, and he doesn't ask for more when I sit back. "I believe you," I say. And I mean it. I really do.

Fran gives me so much crap when Ben comes into the cafe a few days later. She sees how he looks at me, so I can't hide it any longer. When I tell her that we've been 'hanging out', she nearly announces it to the entire shop and offers to buy me a drink to celebrate. She takes full responsibility for our relationship; all I can do is laugh and tune her out as I make coffee.

By next week, Ben and I are dating. He shows me his apartment in Chestnut Hill and it's beautiful. My heart leaps at the three guitars hanging around his living room. I was right. He does play.

He holds me from behind as I scan his entire wall of books. I rest in his arms, but my hand brushes against his scarred wrist. He jerks his hand away.

"I'm sorry-"

"No, it's fine," he says. He cradles his wrist. The bandage has been taken off so now there's a deep scar, rippling with stitches. "I just, I don't want you to touch it. It's gruesome."

I tilt my head. My hand caresses the side of his face. "There's nothing gruesome about you, Ben."

He smiles. But he doesn't say anything else.

—

I'm noticing something... off about Ben. Once while taking a night stroll through Kelly Drive, a half moon high in the sky, he paused while I was talking. His head lifted up, and he closed his eyes. When I asked what was wrong, he replied nothing, and placed his sunglasses on his face.

Another time, a classmate invited me to a party. I didn't want to go alone so Ben came. The entire night, he was attuned to my needs. Every drink I wanted, every awkward conversation I wanted to escape, he was there. It wouldn't have been strange until another guy came to talk to me. Ben appeared out of nowhere and pushed the guy away. Thankfully, the guy wasn't an aggressive type. He let the whole thing go when I apologized.

When I asked Ben why he did that, he only said he was sorry, and that sometimes he gets protective. I was pissed. And it was our first fight.

We didn't talk for an entire day. I went to work. I went home and was itching to call him when I heard guitar plucking from outside my window. He was standing across the street, playing *Little Wing* by Jimi Hendrix. He was bathed under the orange streetlamp, still wearing his leather jacket. Still wearing his sunglasses.

I forgot why I was even mad. I invited him up.

—

Thanksgiving arrives and I want to put that whole thing behind us. My grandma always has dinner at her house in South Philly, and I want Ben to join us. I've never brought anyone home before, so I know this will freak out my family.

When Ben agrees to come, he only says that he has something to do later that night. So, this is really happening. He's meeting my family.

We step off the bus and my grandma's house sits across the street, in the middle of a bunch of rowhomes. Already, I can see my cousins sitting out on the porch.

My feet freeze. I tug at the hem of my red dress. Ben sees me fidgeting. "What's wrong?"

"I don't know if I can do this," I say. "We can go back. Order Chinese?" I'm about to walk in the opposite direction, but Ben catches my arm.

"It's going to be okay." He pats my hat down affectionately then presses his palm against the side of my face. "I want to meet your family."

I twitch my nose and he smiles, still holding my face in his hand. He kisses me. "I never talk about my family. It's not the greatest story. But you always talk about yours and I want to meet them."

I sigh. "Okay, but if they say something offensive, don't say I didn't give you an out."

He laughs and wraps his arm around my shoulder. "I think I'll be okay. But remember I need to leave by eight," he says and slides his sunglasses down on his face.

"Yeah, I remember."

We arrive at my grandma's house and immediately hear a cacophonous cheer. My cousins surround us. Half of them circle me, and the other half circle Ben. They welcome him. They interrogate me. They only give us space when my grandma comes shuffling to the front door.

She's wearing a beige dress with lace decorated at the collar. Her white hair is braided back into a bun and she smiles at me. Her eyes gloss over Ben and she waves. "Come on in."

My mouth waters at the smell of turkey baking in the oven. Cornbread and baked pies give off their scent as well, traveling all the way into the living room. My grandma's house doesn't seem different than one would expect. There are photos on the walls that date back to the early 1900s, along with about a thousand family photos and baby dedications. But it makes Ben stop and stare at them before my grandma turns around.

"Nice to finally meet you, Ben." Her brows suddenly furrow. "Why are you wearing sunglasses inside the house-"

"I'm sorry." Ben removes his glasses. "I forget they're on sometimes." He extends his scarred hand. "Pleasure to finally meet the woman who raised Kiya."

My grandma's eyes widen when she sees his scar. "Good Lord, what happened to you?"

For the first time ever, Ben stutters. He looks at me for help. "Living in Philly, Nan," I say. "Someone got him on the train."

She sizes Ben up and focuses on his Jimi Hendrix shirt for a moment. "I see. Well, dinner will be ready in a few. Go on, sit, get comfortable." She points to a couch.

"Thank you so much," Ben says. He even does a half-bow and the second-hand embarrassment nearly kills me.

"You don't have to bow, boy." Nan isn't going easy on him.

"Right, sorry-"

"*Chile...*" She gives me a look before heading back into the kitchen.

I hold back a laugh when I join him on the couch. "She hates me," he says, stunned.

"She doesn't." I pat his knee. "Just, don't bow. Don't have to be so formal." I laugh.

He chuckles and nods. "No bows. Got it. Don't know what I was thinking."

33

Dinner is bearable, thankfully. Nan and my aunts cook enough to feed an entire village, so no one has a moment to hound Ben and I some more.

I watch Ben charm my aunts with his knowledge of books and music. I get a lot of approving looks from my cousins, but when I glance over at Nan, she's unimpressed.

It gets close to eight and Ben starts to fidget. So, after dessert is passed out, we make our rounds saying goodbye. Ben waits outside on the porch as I say goodbye to Nan.

"You be careful with that one," she says as she hugs me.

"Always, Nan." I kiss her cheek.

I meet Ben outside. His sunglasses are back on his face and he's gazing up into the sky. The full moon is bright, casting white light over the entire porch. "You ready?" I ask.

He snaps from his thoughts. "Oh, yeah." He offers his elbow and we walk to the bus stop.

Ben is quiet on the way home. All I can think about is how he fits in with my family. "You did so well tonight. I mean, you blew it with Nan."

"I blew it?" He seems genuinely hurt and I laugh.

"No, oh my god. You were fine. They loved you."

He smiles and brings my hand to his lips. "Well, it was fun. Thank you."

"What do you have to do tonight?" I ask. "I mean, I was going to ask if you wanted to come over but-"

34

He lifts his sunglasses so I can see his eyes. "You want me to come over? Or like *come over?*"

My face warms and I look out the window. "You know what? Never mind-"

He laughs. "No, Kiya. Come on." His hand lays on my thigh. "I can come over for... maybe a few minutes. But then I have to go."

The warmth doesn't leave my face when I look back at him. It's good enough for me.

My hands jitter as I unlock the door. Ben comes in behind me, and I ask if he wants something to drink. I need something to distract me, but Ben says no. I go to the kitchen anyway and pour a cup of water.

I hear Ben drop his coat over the couch. He saunters into the kitchen and leans on the wall. He lifts his sunglasses on top of his head and grins. "What's wrong with you?"

I set down the untouched water. "Nothing." My voice comes out in a whisper.

He looks at the way I wring my hands and he sighs. "Well, I guess I'll go then." He begins to place the sunglasses back on his face, but I stop him. I gently take the sunglasses from his hands and come closer. And in the next moment, our lips meet. His hand cradles the side of my face.

My arms wrap around his shoulders, and he hugs me closer. A little too close. A little too strong.

My arms loosen around his shoulders. "You're hurting me," I gasp and he releases me.

"Damn it," he whispers. He holds his head as if he's in pain. "Give me a minute?"

I nod and watch as he goes to the bathroom, nearly tripping over himself on the way.

I gulp down that cup of water as I wait. One minute. Then two. Then five.

Suddenly, a crash comes from the bathroom. It sounds like the shelf over the toilet fell. I run to the door. "Ben? Are you okay?"

All I hear is him breathing. I try to open the door, but it barely budges like he's leaning his weight against it. It opens just a crack and when I see him glance through the space, I swear I see red eyes. The door slams shut.

"Ben? The hell? What's going on?"

"...'m fine," he groans. His voice is deeper, and he's speaking as if he's holding his breath. "I'm... having a migraine. Could you get me some aspirin? You're all out."

"Oh," I rest my hand on the door. "Okay, just wait here. I'll go to the corner store."

I grab my keys and glance at the bathroom door again. It's still closed, but I wait a moment, hoping for Ben to come out perfectly fine.

The store on the corner is open for just a few more minutes, so I hurry to get the aspirin. As I walk back, my eyes lift up to the full moon. My stomach feels heavy, and I'm unsure if it's from Nan's food earlier.

Once I'm back at my apartment, I pause before my front door. I fish out my key, but a scratching sound halts me in my tracks. I glance down the hallway and back. It sounds close. I lean forward until my ear is on the door. It's coming from inside.

The door opens slowly. "Ben?"

A streak of light from the lamp pours over the wooden floor, but the rest of the studio is cast in dark shadows. The overhead light is off, but I can still see the outlines of my furniture. My couch. My bed over in the corner. My refrigerator in the kitchen. My... my...

It's a figure standing in the corner between the tv and the window. It looms, nearly touching the ceiling and it has a hand on the blinds. My breath hitches in my throat. The floor seals me in place.

Darkness covers its body, but its long, yellow talons tap on the window. I can hear its breathing, huffing, growling.

I tighten my keys in my hands and take a slow step back, but the floor creaks under my foot. Its head snaps back at me.

Red eyes blaze in the darkness, and I don't waste any time. I run.

My feet trip over themselves, but I push myself up and huff down the hallway. I feel a thud, like a massive boom, clopping behind me. Snarls and growls rev in my ears, and I go silent. I bust through the stairwell. Damn the landlord for not fixing the elevator. I go down the stairs, taking the steps by two.

I hear a clatter a moment later and I can't help but look up. A flash of black hovers at the top of the stairwell. Red eyes latch onto me as its mouth gapes open, unleashing a howl so loud it echoes off the walls.

It suddenly moves, dashing down the steps and my feet move quicker. I'm fully jumping down the steps at this point. Pain shocks my knees as I land on each platform.

A howl roars behind me again, and it makes me lose my footing. I fall down the remainder of the steps.

My ankle and knee get banged up as I roll, but I hurry to my feet, and run like a baby deer taking its first steps.

I'm on the first floor, finally, and I slam the stairwell door shut behind me. I run out of the building into a thick fog that coats all of Germantown Avenue. Street lamps and the full moon are my only source of light as I pat my pockets for my phone, but then I realize. It had to have dropped when I fell.

"Damn it!" My voice shakes as I glance back at my apartment building. My family lives across the city. Fran is the only person I know who lives in Germantown. She lives past the cemetery. With my sore ankle, I limp in her direction.

Suddenly, the sound of metal being crushed echoes through the quiet street. I glance back to see the large, black figure shoot out from my apartment building. Its red eyes gleam above the thick white fog. It howls once more, and my stomach dips.

It takes off, becoming a black blur amidst the fog. It's running towards me, on all fours and I can hear its talons scraping the cobblestone.

My feet move on their own again and go off toward the cemetery. I hope to hide in the fog. Branches snap under my feet as I dive through the cemetery's gate. I slow down and crouch behind the large tombstones. My ankle is throbbing, but it's nothing compared to how my heart is pounding.

I feel the creature before I see it. It enters the cemetery, shaking the ground with each footstep. It stops. It sniffs the air and its large feet shuffle through the dead leaves. I hold my breath and move, hopping to the next tombstone.

If I can get it lost here, I can sneak back out to the main road and go to Fran's house. And then I can call the police.

But then I step on a large branch and my sore ankle buckles. A cry rips through me as I fall to the ground.

Vicious growls fill the cemetery and a dark figure suddenly leaps onto the tombstone above me. The fog clears, and I can finally see its face. Its silhouette stands out against the full moon and its red eyes darken. Its fangs leak putrid saliva and it lands on my forehead. It leans forward and I notice something...

Its clothes are tattered, like they've been stretched to their limit. On its upper body, I see the remnants of a shirt. A Jimi Hendrix shirt.

My voice squeaks. "Ben?"

The creature's growl lowers. Its eyes are still boring into me.

"Is... is that you?"

It doesn't attack. It only looks at me, teeth bared and a growl low in its throat. I struggle to sit up. "How is... how..."

Its hand reaches out to me, slowly, and I study the yellow talons. My eyes trace up its hand until I see its wrist. A deep gash is indented in its fur, scarring the skin underneath.

"Ben," I say. I reach out my hand to rub his scarred wrist. "It's going to be okay."

But as soon as I touch him, he lunges forward. His jaw sinks into my neck.

I'm in... I'm in terrible pain. The full moon hangs in the sky as fog waves around me. It's so quiet, but I can hear cars driving by on the street outside of the cemetery. I'm holding my neck, liquid running over my fingers. I feel... warm. And my eyelids are so, so heavy.

A figure blocks my view of the moon. A man, looming over me, with blood dripping down the front of his shirt.

"B... Ben..." My hand reaches out to him weakly while I still try to keep the wound pressed. My voice strains to get any higher.

Ben kneels to me, brushing my hair from my face. His eyes are glossed with tears. "I'm sorry, Kiya," he says. "I didn't mean for it to be you." He kisses my forehead.

"Help..." I moan. He starts to stand up, but my fingers loosely grip his torn collar. He pries my fingers off easily. "Please..."

"You'll be okay, I promise. It's just... it's your turn now. Find someone else on the next full moon, like I did." He removes the remainder of his torn shirt and presses it against my neck. "You'll be fine."

My hand shakes as I reach out to him again, but Ben steps away. "You'll be fine." He turns his back on me. "I promise, Kiya. You'll be fine."

And I watch him leave, disappearing through the thick fog, leaving me here alone. So terribly alone.

iii. jessica

On the west side of Germantown, I enjoy taking walks with my kids on early afternoons. Well, they aren't *my* kids. I don't think I'll ever want to have any of my own, but they're the kids I nanny. Devan and Kristen are seven and nine, respectively. Our days vary, but we always try to make time to go to the park. I need some way to expel their energy after school.

Today, I pick them up from their bus stop. It rained earlier this morning, but now, there's a muggy mist weighing heavily in the air. Wet brown and yellow leaves clump together on the street.

The bus stops on the corner and Devan jumps down the steps, landing in a small puddle. Water splashes up his rain boots. He runs over to me. Kristen is right behind him. She has her hood up, her attention focused on a book as she walks.

"Miss Jess!" Devan calls. In one hand he has a stack of half eaten Twizzlers and in the other a skeleton toy. "We had a Halloween party today." When he talks, his tongue is blue.

"Oh, so cool!" I record a video of him showing off his toy. "Did you get that from the party?"

"Yeah, I won it in musical chairs," Devan smiles at the camera. Two of his front teeth are missing.

I pan the camera over to Kristen. "Any fun things today, Kris?"

She only shrugs and turns the page.

"Okay..." I turn the camera off.

Nannying is my main source of income, but I also run a vlog about Devan and Kristen. It does pretty well and their parents receive a percentage from any brand deals I get.

We walk down the street. Kristen is in front still reading her book. I want to ask her what she's reading, but I know better than to interrupt her when she gets like this. Devan holds my hand, telling me about his day and I swing our hands lazily.

Devan's in the middle of telling me about his Halloween costume when I see a man walking up the path. His arms are stiffly by his side. He has bright blonde hair that's neatly combed back and he's wearing a blue sweater vest with tan slacks. He's not wearing a coat which I think is weird.

Kristen is still nose-deep in her book, and they're on a course for collision. She doesn't look like she plans on getting out of the way.

The man stares straight ahead, wearing a thin smile. His eyes are glossed over like no one is home. He doesn't even blink. He and Kristen get closer, and he doesn't step out of the way. He bumps into Kristen and her book flies out of her hand.

"Hey!" I shout.

The man doesn't stop. He doesn't apologize. And as he passes us, I'm hit with an overwhelming smell of soap. It's so strong, it almost stinks. He keeps walking, as if we weren't even there.

We stare after him as he continues down the block. "Asshole!" I call out to him. I pick up Kristen's book, and the cover is wet. "Sorry, Kris."

"It's okay," she says. She puts the book in her backpack.

"That guy was mean," Devan says. He holds my hand again.

"Yeah," I say. We keep walking. "Don't tell your parents I called him an asshole, though."

Kristen walks in step with us. "But he *was* an asshole."

"Hey," I nudge her, and they both laugh.

"Hey, can I say it?" Devan asks. He shakes my hand in anticipation. "Please? Kristen said it-"

"Okay, okay, fine. Go nuts."

"Asshole!" Devan yells to the misty sky.

"Okay, enough," I laugh, shaking my head.

We reach their house and the rest of our day goes as normal. I fix them a snack. We work on their homework and watch a movie until their dad comes home.

As I'm packing up to leave, I see Devan going around the living room, searching the cushions and tossing pillows out of the way.

"What's wrong?" I ask.

"My skeleton. The one I won. I can't find it."

I think back to the afternoon. I realize that I don't remember seeing it in the house. "Did you drop it on the walk home?"

Devan's shoulders deflate and he groans. I stifle a laugh. He's so very dramatic. "I did! I think I did," he whines. "When that man bumped into Kristen. Oh, now I'll never see it again."

"Okay, okay. On my way home, I'll look for it, okay?"

Devan perks up immediately and hugs me. "Thank you, Miss Jess!"

I say my goodbyes and Mr. O'Donnell gives me a twenty-dollar cash tip. I like when he comes home before Mrs. O'Donnell. He always gives me a little something for my troubles. The reasoning for this tip was Halloween. He tells me to use it to get a drink or something and have fun.

I pocket the money and head home. I live in Germantown, too. My great aunt, Florence, owns a pretty big house on Pastorius and she invited me to live with her when I was eighteen. My parents had just discovered that I was gay and wanted me as far away from them as possible. Aunt Florence, who insists I call her Flo, has been nothing but kind.

She's very artsy. She directs plays in Chestnut Hill and Brooklyn, so she's always traveling. But when she's home, she fills up the space and makes me feel welcomed.

On my way home, I go down McCallum Street where we saw that man. I scan along the manicured sidewalk and rose bushes, but Devan's skeleton doll isn't there.

He'll be okay. He has tons of toys.

I put my headphones on and continue my walk home. The sun sets and golden hour shines on the houses, bathing them in light. I'm thinking about how I will edit my next video when I suddenly smell... soap. It's strong, like someone is holding a lathered bar of it under my nose.

I take out an earbud and footsteps sound behind me. I look back and nearly freeze in my tracks. The man from earlier is coming down the path. He's still wearing that plain smile. Still looking straight ahead. Still not wearing a coat despite it being chilly outside. And he's still wearing a sweater vest, but this time it's brown and he's got on black slacks instead of tan.

He's walking down the middle of the sidewalk, taking up space on both sides. I step out of the way to wait for him to pass. He doesn't even acknowledge me.

The closer he gets, I notice his face is a bit different. His eyes are softer. His lips are a bit fuller. Even his blonde hair is styled differently. He actually looks... younger.

He passes by me, and I have to hold my breath. The soap smell fills the air.

I watch him head down the street and I follow after him. I probably shouldn't have let him pass. I'm only half a block behind him, and I can still smell faint traces of soap. My eyes stay on him as I put my headphones back on.

He turns onto Pastorius Street and I slow down. I have to turn there, too, but I don't want to seem like I'm following him.

I cross the street so that he's on the other side and I see him passing behind the parked cars. His walk is even-keeled. He doesn't slow down. He doesn't speed up. He doesn't falter to the left or right. His pace is just the same. He never breaks his stride.

My house is coming up and even though he doesn't see me, I don't want him to glance back and see where I live.

I don't have to worry about that though because he suddenly turns into a driveway. It's the empty house for sale directly across from mine. The house is huge. One bored night, I looked up the asking price and it's almost half a million.

The young man walks onto the wraparound porch and goes inside.

When I get to my porch, I pretend I'm checking the mail so I can stall for a minute and look across the street. The house, if I remember correctly, has five bedrooms, two and a half baths, finished upstairs and attic. There aren't any curtains blocking the large bay window which looks into the dining room. There's a table that wasn't there before, decorated with a flower vase. And at the table are three people, including the man I saw earlier.

The young man comes into view, and he joins them at the table. Two women sit across from him and are alike in the same way the two men are. Both women have blonde hair, too. One is styled in a very 1950's fashion. I don't know how else to describe it. It's pinned up, off of her shoulders. The other woman, the one who looks younger, has a ponytail that rests down her back. And like the identical men, they're wearing sweater vests too. The older wearing purple and the younger wearing pink.

And they're all sitting there, looking at each other. Not moving. It doesn't even look like they're talking. They're just... smiling.

I go inside my house.

"Jessica," my great aunt calls when I enter. "I was just about to call you."

"Hey," I say. I look through the front window, trying to look into the house across the street, but it's too far. "Did you know a family moved into the big house?"

"The one across the street? It's been on the market for ages."

"Yeah, the family that moved in looks really weird," I say. I'm still trying to get a glimpse from the front room, but I give up. I finally look at Flo, and she's dressed in a loudly printed dress. Her gray hair is covered with a matching scarf.

She fixes the thick red glasses on her face, they match her lipstick, and she shakes her head. "You can't call people weird these days. They're just different." She slings her large purse over her shoulder. "You should know, sweet Jessica."

I roll my eyes. "Not weird like that. They're just... I don't know."

"Well, if you cross paths with them, make yourself friendly." She kisses my forehead. Her floral perfume hits my nose and reminds me of that guy's soapy smell.

"Yeah, no. I'm not gonna do that." I wipe the lipstick stain from my head. "And where are you going so late, Miss Flo?"

She chuckles. "Please. Eight is hardly late. But if you must know, I'm meeting my co-director to discuss our new show in Brooklyn. Just a few drinks."

"Okay, well, be safe." I smile and she grins at me.

"Oh, darling, I'm never careful. You know that." She heads out the door. "Make sure you lock up, Jessica."

I heat some leftovers for dinner and spend the rest of the night in my room reviewing footage from the day. I start a new post for my nanny blog, but then exit out of it. I can't focus. Maybe it's a sign I need to go to bed.

In the bathroom, I stare in the mirror and brush my teeth. A window faces the front of the house and I glance out. I've never really noticed that I can see the big house so clearly from here, but then again, I didn't care before.

The lights are lit on the first floor of the house, but I can't see inside. I'm too far away. It dawns on me that I'm still spying on these people, so I turn back to brushing my teeth.

Before I turn around, I hear the front door of their house open. Our street is pretty quiet, cars roam by every so often, so I can hear someone stepping out of the house.

It's one of the women. The...older one, I think. Yeah, she is wearing a purple sweater vest and her hair is pinned up. She walks just like the men, her shoulders a bit hunched by her ears and her pace so unnaturally even.

I watch her leave her porch. She doesn't even look both ways before crossing the street. It looks like she's carrying something in her hand, but I can't tell what it is.

She disappears from my line of sight, and I think that's the end of it when I hear two knocks thud downstairs.

"Shit!" I turn off the bathroom light.

I hear the knocks again. *Boom. Boom.*

It's quiet. I kneel underneath the window, waiting in the darkness. I grip my wet brush, holding it like it's some kind of protection.

After a few seconds pass, I slowly rise.

The woman is standing there. In the middle of the street. And she's looking up at me. A wide smile on her face. With one finger, she points at me and then down to the front door.

She then turns on her heels and walks back to her house.

I keep the lights off as I wait downstairs. I hear Flo's keys jiggle in the front door, and I meet her at the threshold.

"Oh, Jessica!" She reeks of alcohol. "Waited up for Ol' Great Aunt Flo?"

"Just wanted to make sure you were okay."

Flo comes in and I hover by the front door, glancing over to the house across the street. The lights are off now.

"I had a wonderful time. We have a house to start production, but I'll be going to Brooklyn for a few days. Oh, this was at the front door." Flo turns around and she's holding a skeleton doll. Devan's skeleton doll.

"I have no idea who put it there," Flo says. Her words are slurring.

"I do." I take the doll from her. "Come on, let's get you to bed."

"Oh, you, dear, are just the *sweetest little lesbian.*" She tries to pat my face and nearly cuts me with one of her many rings.

"I know. You always tell me when you're drunk." I start walking her up to her room.

"Darling, a lady never gets drunk-"

"-she gets spirited." I finish her infamous phrase. "I know."

—

Devan is over the moon when I bring him his skeleton doll. I don't tell him how I got it. I don't even want to think about that weird family. And thankfully when I left this morning, I didn't run into them or see them.

It's a cool morning, so I take Devan and Kristen to the park. They play with a few kids from the neighborhood, and I sit on the bench and watch. I'm on the phone with my girlfriend, Nicole. She's telling me about her boss whom she hates.

"What's up with you?" she asks suddenly and it snaps me from my thoughts. "I'm telling you some really good stuff. Great tea. It's piping hot and you're just... bleh."

"Oh, sorry. Just been seeing some weird things lately. This family moved into the house across the street-"

"Damn, the one that costs half a mill?"

I laugh. "How do you know that?"

"I look up all the houses in your neighborhood. Even yours. That's how I know Miss Flo got money."

"Anyway," I chuckle. "Yeah, that house. But the family is so weird. They're all the same. Like they all dress the same. I'd understand if it was like a cultural thing, but they're white. They're all wearing the same fuckin' sweater vest. It's so weird."

"Yeah, that's weird. Just try to avoid them," is Nicole's only advice.

"I'm trying my best to."

Apparently, I don't try *that* hard to avoid them, because when we leave the park, I see them again.

I'm holding Devan's hand and Kristen is walking ahead of us. She isn't reading this time but has headphones on, listening to an audiobook.

The weird family is walking up the street, and I preemptively corral Devan and Kristen to one side of the path.

The older man is in the front, then the older woman is beside him. The younger versions of themselves are in tow and they move in sync. The swing of their arms and stride are perfectly matched. And I didn't notice until now, but they're all the exact same height.

When they pass us, I put myself between them and the kids. We wait by the edge of the sidewalk until they pass. The

52

family seamlessly moves into a single line. They pass us one by one, all of them reeking of fresh soap. And as they pass, they don't look straight ahead. No.

Each one looks me dead in the eye. Their faces are pulled into that sickening smile. It sends chills up my spine.

They stop at the corner, and a city bus pulls up. They climb on.

"They look weird, right?" Kristen says.

"You can't call people weird," I say. We go back to their house.

I leave the O'Donnells almost as soon as we get there. Their parents are home on the weekends, so I take the kids out to play on Sundays. I wave to their mom who's busy on a work call, and their dad walks me out. He gives me another twenty dollars.

On the walk home, I have to skirt around trash bins and recycling. It only reminds me that I have to bring the trash out front, and I'm dreading it.

When I get to my street, my attention is glued to the house across from mine. It's been a couple of days since I've first seen them. I haven't seen a single moving truck or car in their driveway. Wouldn't they have furniture? And why would they be taking a bus if they spent half a million dollars on a house? It didn't make sense. And I just couldn't ignore the strangeness.

I get to my house and bring the trash out front. Once I push it to the sidewalk, I notice trash bags across the street.

Three evenly sized bags sit on the curb in front of the large house. I glance into their large window, and they still haven't put up any curtains. The table is still there, but that's it. No other furniture. No paintings or pictures. Nothing.

Curiosity finds me crossing the street. I had just seen them taking the bus so they shouldn't be home.

I glance up and down the block to ensure I'm not being watched. The trash bags aren't tied tightly so they open easily. I'm met with a strong odor of soap again and when I look inside the bag, my mouth drops.

It's filled with paper. Pages from magazines and newspapers are balled up. Sheets of fresh clean paper are torn and discarded. "What the fuck?"

I look into the other trash bags and it's the same thing. Random bits of paper made to look like trash.

"Jessica?"

I jump and turn, finding Flo standing there across the street. She stands in front of her car, her door still ajar. She takes off her sunglasses and gapes at me. "What on earth?"

"Uh," I look down at the open bag of trash in my hand. "No, wait, Aunt Flo." I tie up the bags again. Flo shakes her head when I meet her on the sidewalk. "I can explain."

"Trash-digging?" She hums. "I thought you knew better." She goes back to her car to gather her purse.

"No, that family is weird. They don't even have real trash." I pause when Flo looks at me and suddenly realize how crazy I sound.

We go into the house and Flo flops on the couch. She kicks her shoes off. "Jessica, you're worrying me."

"You're worried?" I point out the front window towards the big house. "There's something off about that family. I keep seeing them around. They... they smell like soap," my words stumble and Flo sits up to look at me. "They all look the same. They're always smiling. They're just weird."

Silence fills the living room, and I can't tell what Flo is thinking. She clips her glasses in her shirt. "So let me get this straight. This newly arrived family is weird because you keep seeing them even though we live across from them," she counts the transgressions on her fingers, "They smell like soap?" she says in the form of a question. "They look the same and they smile." She holds up four fingers. "Am I missing anything else?"

A deep sigh rolls out of me. I know I sound crazy. "And they're tall."

Flo laughs. "And they're tall?" She throws her hands up. "Dearest Jessica, I never thought someone of your caliber would be so closed-minded. Now, I saw that family and you're right, they look a bit the same and they're tall, but they look European. Maybe they're from Norway? Have you talked to them?"

"Well, no-"

"Darling," Flo stands from the couch. She cups my face with her hands. "Xenophobia does not bode well with you. Neither does this frantic state of mind. I'm worried I won't be able to go to Brooklyn tonight. You're obviously under duress-"

"I'm fine, Flo." I pull her hands from my face. "You're right. I'm just spiraling and maybe my imagination got the best of me."

Flo twitches her nose as she thinks to herself. "Very well. I'm going to get ready to leave. Perhaps that beautiful girlfriend of yours would like to come over for... a nightcap, maybe?"

"God, Aunt Flo. Stop."

She laughs as she goes up to her room.

Despite Flo's joke, I actually call Nicole to come over. It feels good that after fretting all day, we can lay on the couch together and watch *Hocus Pocus*.

I tell Nicole all about the family and what I found in their trash. After what Flo said, Nicole can see where she's coming from. She even mentions how I would say certain things to her when we first dated about her Jamaican customs. So I agree, maybe I'm going a little crazy. But I still feel deep inside that I'm not. For my sanity, I choose to let it go.

Nicole has to wake up early tomorrow for work, so she can't stay the night. We finish watching our movie, we eat, and I walk her to her car.

She's parked in the driveway, but I can't help but look across the street again. The lights are off.

"I can stay," Nicole says. She leans on her car door. "You still look like you've seen a ghost."

"We just watched a scary movie."

"Hocus Pocus is *not* a scary movie," she laughs. She fixes the string on my hoodie. "I'm serious. If this thing with your neighbors is..." she looks across the street at the house. "I mean I get it. I think it's still weird, but maybe it's just one of those things where you see weird people and move on. They aren't hurting anyone."

I think about how they brought back Devan's toy. Maybe they weren't bad after all. Just different. "Yeah, I guess you're right."

A raindrop falls on my forehead and then my lip. "Ugh, I hate driving in the rain." Nicole groans and she hops into the car. She rolls down the window and I bend down. "Call me if you need me, okay? For anything."

"I will." I kiss her then stand back as she rolls up the window. Rain starts to fall more, but I don't mind. I wave and watch her back out of the driveway.

Once she's gone, I look at the empty house one last time before heading back inside.

It's pretty late, so I clean up the living room, shower, and edit a few videos for the vlog before turning in for bed. The rain is in full force now and it soothes me to sleep.

—

I wake up with an intense urge to pee, but for some reason, I lie there, staring at the ceiling. Rain trickles down my window and the sound is soothing. I'm not sure what time it is, but I like these late hours of the night. It's so peaceful.

I finally sit up and when I look in the corner of my room, my blood runs cold. The space between my window and closet

is unusually dark. And it looks like the outline of a head...
maybe shoulders hunched up-

I turn the bedside lamp on. My heart beats loudly in my
ears.

There's nothing there.

I sigh and slide out of bed.

I use the bathroom and when I wash my hands, the floor
beneath the window glistens. The window is open. When I
close it, I sneak a glance at the house across the street. I don't
want to seem like I'm looking for them. It just so happens that
I'm looking out the window and the house is there.

The lights are still off. Maybe they went away for the night?

When I close the window, I realize I haven't locked up. Flo
would kill me if she knew I forgot.

The hallway is dark as I head down. At the top of the stairs,
I smell something with a strong odor. It's strange.

Flo's house normally smells like her. Like flowers, or maybe
apple cinnamon in the fall months, but no, this isn't that smell.
It's faint. It smells like soap.

I silently make my way down the steps, and the smell is
getting stronger. Once I reach the bottom, I hear a clang from
the kitchen. A wall divides the living and dining room and I
press my back against it. I hold my breath.

The clanging continues. It sounds like dishes crashing to
the floor. Pots and pans being cast aside.

I slide down and peer over the wall. From down here, I
look into the dining room and have a limited view of the
kitchen. Four figures stand in the darkness, all equal in height.

Two of them are in the kitchen, rifling through the cabinets. Two others are in the dining room, tossing books out of Flo's grand bookcase.

My eyes shut. I rest my head against the wall. *What the fuck, what the fuck, what the fuck, what the fuck do I do?*

My phone is upstairs, but Flo's house phone... Yes, thank you, Flo, for being old school. She keeps it on the little table in the living room. I can see it from where I'm crouched on the floor. I just need to grab it without them seeing.

A loud crash sounds in the kitchen, and I look over the edge again. All four of them convene in the kitchen, and I make my move to grab the phone.

The living room closet is the perfect place to hide, and I dive in without making a noise. I crack the door open so I can see the numbers to dial 911. They answer immediately.

"Someone broke into my house," I whisper into the receiver. "Please, help-" I stop. I see a tall silhouette through the crack lurking closer to the door. "They're here... they-"

The door swings open and the scent of soap fills the closet. I look up at the man. The one with the blue sweater vest. A smile stretches across his face. The phone drops from my hand.

He looks over his shoulder at the rest of his family slowly walking into the living room. All of them enter in sync, all with the same swing of their arms.

He nods his head toward the front door and just like that, he leaves. The family follows after him, each of them smiling. They look straight ahead, as if I weren't even there.

Once they leave, I pick the phone back up and hurry to lock the front door.

"Hello," the dispatch answers. "What's happening now?"

"They left," I say, very dumbfounded. "They just left out the door."

"Are you safe?"

"I... I think so."

"Would you like an officer to be sent out?"

I answer immediately. *"Hell yes."*

The police come in no time, and I tell them everything. From the moment I saw the man bump into Kristen, to the woman leaving Devan's toy on the porch, everything. I walk them through the house, detailing the items they tossed on the floor and what they broke. Books and knick-knacks are scattered on the ground, and I can only think about Flo's precious things.

Nicole comes through the door like a bat out of hell and swallows me in a hug. "God, Jess. Are you okay?" She's dressed in her pajamas. Her bonnet is still on her head.

"Yeah, just shaken up."

"I'm so sorry I left."

"I'm glad you did."

She hugs me again, close to tears. "Did they find them?" She looks through the front window where police surround the house across the street. All of the lights are on.

"They're checking for them now."

They search for an hour, but no one is there. The house is abandoned. They contact the realtor and they say the house never sold. No one has expressed interest in it for over a year.

Nicole corroborates my story with the police.

When Flo finally returns, she holds me and never lets me go. She tells the police that she saw them when she was leaving for work the other night.

I don't know what happened to that family or if they just left. I wish I had recorded them when I was with Devan and Kristen, so I had physical proof that these people actually existed. So I know I wasn't imagining everything.

I just know that they're out there. Somewhere. The weird family from across the street.

iv. esme

Life in my mid-twenties had been draining, flat, and colorless. There was no love life to be had but not for lack of suitors. My relationships would always end because we wanted different things. When I met my best friend, Kesi, my life changed for the better, and he pulled me from the brink of depression too many times to count.

When I moved out of my parents' house, I was young, fresh-faced, and determined to cultivate the life I'd planned in my head since childhood. I escaped a home where my family always told me I was always the starter, never the finisher. I had to break away to finally be free to make my own choices.

Kesi and I worked at the same tech startup in Germantown, and I knew I liked him when I excitedly introduced myself on my first day.

"Oh, you must be *really, really* new to tech," he said.

"How can you tell?" I asked.

"Easy. It hasn't robbed you of your joy yet."

After conversing through thin cubicle walls for a few weeks, Kesi and I became good friends. Soon after, he introduced me to Yasmine, his childhood friend, and she welcomed me with open arms.

Kesi and Yasmine grew up in the same Germantown neighborhood and never left. Yasmine was a drop-dead gorgeous Somali woman who modeled doing commercial, and sometimes high-end, shoots. When we first hung out together, I watched how Kesi and Yasmine joked and felt a little like the odd man out. At work the following day, I asked Kesi if he had ever tried to shoot his shot with her. He said he wanted to, a long time ago, but the moment had passed. Besides, Yasmine was focused on chasing her dreams and chose to be single.

Yasmine's career flourished over the years and one night, she announced that she had landed the modeling contract of her dreams. The only drawback was that it would permanently move her to New York. My heart broke at the news, but when I looked at Kesi, he smiled and wrapped her in a crushing hug.

After the news, I noticed a change in Kesi. He threw himself into work, focusing on developing an app that helped users find unmetered residential street parking. I would ask if he wanted to hang out, since Yasmine was busy getting ready to move, and he'd just say no. He always had to work.

The day came when we had to say goodbye to Yasmine. Kesi and I came to her boxed up apartment and she ordered food. We sat up all night, talking, drinking, and reminiscing over the crazy times we had. We laughed, but every time the dust settled, we stewed just for a moment, knowing that everything was about to change.

As we were leaving, Yasmine told us New York was just a train ride away and to not be strangers. I hugged her tightly and said I'd take her up on it. My birthday was coming up and she suggested we come to celebrate. After a night of suppressing tears, it was a nice thing to look forward to.

I waited down the hall as Kesi and Yasmine stood outside her door. Kesi's tall body leaned on Yasmine's chest and he cried, clutching her desperately. I could hear Yasmine shushing him, rubbing the back of his head, and telling him it would be okay. I wondered how it felt. To have someone who was a part of your life for so long be ripped away like that. I hoped to never to feel that kind of pain.

Kesi and I walked together to our bus stop in silence. He sniffed every few seconds, and I felt he was embarrassed for how he acted. If anything, it just made me like him more.

We sat on the bench, relishing in the cool October night. I broke the silence and we ended up talking about the first day we met. I wasn't sure if it was the wine, but I snuggled beside him. I laid my head on his shoulder, laughing at his dramatic account of our first meeting.

"I'm pretty sure I wasn't trying to get into your pants, you liar." I laughed.

He shrugged and my head bumped against his shoulder. "Okay, maybe not," he said. "I thought you were kind of cute, though. Your optimism, I mean. Like who's that excited to work?" His neck craned to look at me, and I stared into his eyes. His attention flitted to my lips for a brief second and my stomach dropped.

I sat up and scooted until there was space between us. He didn't say anything and pulled out his phone.

"Hm, I never knew you felt that way," I said as nonchalantly as I could.

He shrugged again, scrolling his phone. "I mean, it was like seven years ago. I'm not holding a flame for you, Esme, so it doesn't really matter." He scratched his dark, full beard in thought. He glanced over and I must've looked offended because he threw his arm over my shoulder. "Aw, but you're still my girl, Es." He rubbed my head. "What was in that wine, Yas!" He yelled to the quiet sky. "It got me feelin' *emotional* tonight."

I pushed his arm off of me. "Stop, you ass." I fixed my hair and when I looked across the street, I thought I saw something black on two little legs diving into the bushes. "Did you see that?"

Kesi followed my gaze. "See what?"

The bus came careening around the corner and Kesi stood. "Come on."

I stood a little dumbfounded, still looking at the bushes.

"You good?" he asked once we got on the bus.

I kept looking outside, but once I saw it was too dark to see anything, I let it go. Maybe it was like a dog or cat or something. "Yeah, I'm good."

We rode in silence but he sighed when we neared my stop. "Look," he said. "I know we were celebrating Yas tonight, but I have some news, too." He cradled his phone in his hand as he spoke. He nervously jittered his leg.

"Oh, what news?"

"I got an offer for the app." He smiled grimly.

"Oh, that's amazing, Kesi." I pushed his arm. "Why do you look so sad about it? It's not like you have to move away, right?" I chuckled, but stopped when he didn't respond. "Are you moving away?"

"No," he answered quickly. He smiled to put me at ease, but it didn't help. "I'm happy, I am. I just had to sacrifice a lot to make it happen."

I thought back on the past few weeks where he secluded himself. "Yeah, but it paid off, right? Now, you can reap the benefits." My stop was coming up and I pulled the line. I looked at Kesi's pensive face and held his jaw in my hand. "You deserve it, Kesi. You did a great job."

He patted my hand on his face. "Thanks, Es."

I got off the bus, and Kesi waved sadly. I didn't know where this melancholy guy came from, but I didn't like it.

—

October 31st finally made its appearance, and although I wasn't ecstatic about being another year older, I was excited to see Yasmine. Since the night we said goodbye, I saw Kesi three times outside of work. He said he was busy doing another project, which took up most of his time. But at work, I'd find him sleeping at his desk or completely distracted when talking to him.

I told Yasmine about it and she only said that when he gets a great idea, he could really hole himself away. I knew Kesi, maybe not as much as Yasmine, but I knew he was hiding something.

My birthday was a time to cut loose and hang with Yasmine. Kesi said he was coming along to New York the night we made plans, but he never mentioned meeting up to take the train.

It ended up not being of consequence, because Yasmine had to cancel.

"Aw, babe, I'm so sorry. I'm just sick over missing this," Yasmine whined on the phone. She was scheduled for a photo shoot and had to be flown out to Miami early tomorrow morning. She told them that she couldn't, but her agent said she already agreed to it months ago.

It broke my heart that I couldn't see her, but I didn't let on. I blinked away tears and put on a smile. "Oh, it's fine. I can just do something here."

"Maybe you and Kesi could-"

"Yeah, maybe not." I sighed. "You know, ever since you left, he's been acting so aloof. I know he's worried about this app, but I don't know. I'm worried about him."

Yasmine grew quiet. "Yeah, I didn't say anything because I was in the middle of moving, and everything that day was so crazy. But when he left, he said he was sorry. I thought he was apologizing for crying, but he seemed troubled by something else."

I thought about that night, too. He *was* crying a lot.

"Just keep an eye on him. Force him to go out with you tonight," she said. She perked up, and her voice turned bubbly. "Oh, Es, I forgot. One of the girls I model with is a partial owner of some new upscale club in Philly. You and Kesi should go for sure. It's called The Underground. Let me know how it goes."

Once we hung up, I scrolled through reviews and web photos of The Underground. The name was deceiving as hell. I thought the place would look seedy and trashy, but the photos showed plush velvet seating, an immaculate bar with chandeliers, and an oversized dance floor. It was beautiful. The dress code was stringent, so I knew I'd have to pull out our best. *We'd* have to pull our best. I had to call Kesi.

He answered almost immediately which was a bit of a shock. "Oh, hey, Es." He sounded out of breath. "Happy birthday."

"Oh, thanks," I said. "Um, Yas had to cancel. Big shoot in Miami tomorrow."

"Aw, damn." He huffed into the receiver. "I wanted to see her."

"I know. Me, too." I listened to his labored breathing. "Are you okay?"

"Yeah, I'm good. What's up with you?"

I blinked. "Oh, well. We could still go out if you want. It's okay if-"

"No, Es. I want to. Let's go out. Your pick."

"Yas knows someone who owns a club downtown. We could go there-"

Kesi suddenly shouted, and it sounded like his phone had fallen.

"Kes!" I gripped the phone. "What- What's happening? Are you okay?"

"Yeah," Kesi came back. He took a deep breath. "Sorry, I'm uh... jogging. Busted my ass in front of all these people."

I hold back my smile. "Are you good?"

"I'm good," he teased. "I know you want to laugh."

"I don't!"

"Yeah, whatever. I'll pick you up tonight."

I shook my head, feeling a bit better that he sounded normal. "I'll see you tonight."

—

I rummaged through my closet and found a sexy red dress I'd bought a few years back. Holding it up to my brown skin, I did a little spin. This was going to be a head-turning Halloween birthday for me. My shoulder-length chunky twists pulled into a high ponytail and a simple gold necklace completed the look. I decided against the hoops and went with my small studs. Less was more.

Around ten, Kesi phoned to tell me the car share was outside. I opened the window, and a cool breeze forced the hair on my arms to stand on end. The houses across the street were decorated for Halloween. Kids were walking up and down the sidewalk, swinging their candy buckets.

I peeked down and saw Kesi standing outside the car with white roses in hand. He wore a black button-up shirt and fitted slacks. He adjusted his neckline as he waited for me. Seeing him stand there, waving to the trick-or-treaters that peppered the block, my heart yearned for him. Not in a romantic way. I just really missed my friend these past weeks.

I grabbed my purse and hurried out. He greeted me with a huge smile and a hug. I breathed in his cologne and pulled him in tight. I wanted to stay there a moment longer, but then he stepped back, offering the white roses.

"Happy birthday, Es," he said warmly. "And um, wow. Who are you and what have you done with my friend, Esme?" He lifted my arm to get a better look at my dress.

"Oh, stop. Look at you? I've never seen you like this before. You look very handsome, very debonair."

He beamed, then began striking model-like poses. I chuckled. "Let's have a great birthday night, shall we?" he asked, opening the car door.

We pulled up to a historic-looking building a few moments later. It stood alone on the block surrounded by an iron fence gate. It looked more like an old styled home than a nightclub.

I looked at the address that Yasmine sent me. "This *is* the place." The sidewalk was empty. I was surprised that a place this fancy didn't have a line wrapping around the corner.

I looked over at Kesi, and he went completely still. His eyes were fixed on the entrance of the club. *The Underground* was written in white lights above the front doors. Gold stanchions with red velvet ropes sat on the porch. Two burly bouncers stood there dressed in black.

We hopped out of the car and Kesi's mouth opened and closed. "What is wrong with you?" I asked.

Kesi fit his hands in his pockets. "I don't think this is a good idea. I think we should leave." He turned around, but our car had already driven off.

"There's nowhere else to go." I shrugged and put my phone back in my purse. "We look great and Yas said this was a good place. I promise. I saw the pictures online. Very swanky."

I hooked my arm through his. "Come on. If it looks weird, we'll leave, okay?"

Kesi blew air from his mouth and nodded. He didn't say anything else.

Walking up to the entrance, a man wearing a red devil mask approached the bouncers. He had two horns jutting from the top of his head. I glanced at Kesi and he looked completely unfazed. The bouncers let the man inside.

"That man had horns," I said to Kesi.

"It's Halloween. What do you expect?"

We stopped in front of the bouncers and they stiffened their stance. The one on the left was taller and burlier than the one on the right. He had short, cropped hair, a full mouth, and a prominent nose. He definitely commanded my attention. He was strikingly handsome.

"Kesi," he said. Before I could say anything, he looked at me. "Esme."

"How do you know our names?" I asked.

"We knew you were coming, luv," his voice rumbled low and the pet name melted my skin. His accent helped the swooning effect, too. His dark eyes fell on Kesi. "Back again? Are you mental?" He chuckled.

Kesi huffed. "Are we allowed in or not?"

The bouncer chuckled and stepped out of the way. "Always welcomed, bruv."

"It's Invite Only tonight," the other bouncer said. He was obviously American. "Closed off to the public."

"They aren't the public." His white teeth glinted when he smiled at me. "They're VIP. Follow me, luv."

The American bouncer raised his brow as we passed. We followed the big man inside.

For a moment, I thought we had the wrong place. We walked into a sitting room, adorned with old mid-1800s furniture and a man stood behind a small bar, fashioning a drink for a man at the counter. But the bouncer directed us past them and led us down a small flight of steps to a heavy metal door. When the bouncer opened it, sound poured out. Alternating red and blue lights flooded over us.

"Welcome to The Underground."

The club was just as beautiful as the photos had illustrated. Brent Faiyaz serenaded us as we walked through. Palpable electricity buzzed in the air, sending a tingling sensation all over my body. People were mildly celebrating Halloween with an assortment of simple props. Masks, fairy wings, convoluted horns, and stylized makeup scattered the club. We snaked through the crowd of modelesque men and women enjoying their Friday night.

The bouncer led us to our own small booth with a bottle of champagne on ice and a bouquet of flowers that put the ones Kesi got for me to shame. I placed my white roses beside them. The bouncer took my hand, helped me to my seat, and bowed when I sat.

"Name's Booker. If you need anything, don't hesitate." He reached for my hand again and kissed the back. My skin flared with heat.

Kesi huffed again, and I honestly forgot he was there for a moment. Booker's face changed completely. His thick lips thinned into a line when he addressed him. "Don't get on too well tonight. There's work to do."

Kesi didn't say a word. He and Booker engaged in a silent stare-off until Booker laughed, his voice booming. He slapped Kesi on the shoulder and jostled him a bit. "Cheers, mate." Booker walked off, moving like a tall, black pillar in the crowd.

"What was that?" I said plainly, but Kesi was still staring down Booker until he disappeared. "Hello? Kesi?"

Kesi finally turned his head to me. "I can explain-"

"You've been here before. When? How?"

He held his hand up in surrender. "Wait, Es." He sighed. "I wanted to wait to say anything, but that offer I got for the app? The owner of The Underground is the one who wants it."

I looked around the club. At the bartenders behind the counter. At the people dancing in costumes on the floor. "Is it, I don't know, shady? Is that why you've been hiding it?"

"No," he said immediately, but then he stopped to think about it. I didn't like that pause.

A masked man appeared out of thin air, sporting a set of thick, twisted horns. They looked heavy on his head. I searched for the strap holding them in place and couldn't find one. He asked for drink requests, and I told him my order. Kesi didn't want anything.

"We can leave," I said once the waiter left. "You look spooked, so-"

"I'm not spooked," Kesi snapped and blinked when he realized he'd yelled at me. "Sorry, maybe we should go." He scanned over the crowd of dancing, sweating people. I wasn't sure what he was looking at. "I'm gonna use the bathroom real quick. I'll be back." He slid from the booth.

By the time I laid eyes on Kesi again, I was working on my second drink. The room was slightly spinning as I made my way out of the booth. Kesi was at the bar, shirt unbuttoned and obviously drunk. I stumbled through the dance floor trying, and failing, to keep my eyes on Kesi. I didn't want to lose him in the crowd.

I bumped into a masked man who was whispering into a woman's ear. I mouthed an apology as I tried to push forward. His face twisted into a deep scowl and he bore long white teeth. The eyes of his mask were two empty black holes and I jumped back. The woman on his arm cackled.

It felt like I blinked a million times. I stared into the masked man's face to see if I'd imagined his long teeth. But when I did, he looked like a normal man. I was just as drunk as Kesi.

I straightened myself up, adjusted the slit of my dress, and looked around again. My eyes landed on Booker. Kesi's arm was thrown around his neck and they were walking towards the back of the club.

I yelled for Kesi, but the music drowned out my voice. They disappeared behind a heavy steel door.

I went to the bartender and shouted above the music. "Hi, I'm looking for Booker." The bartender gave me a disinterested stare while cleaning a glass. "I saw him leave through that door with my friend, Kesi. You know where they went?"

His brow raised at the sound of Kesi's name, then a smile crept onto his face, stretching wider and wider. He motioned for me to come closer, and he spoke low into my ear.

"If Mr. Kesi is with Booker, you won't be seeing him for the rest of the night." He took a deep breath and he blinked, showing his pupils were actually slits. "You're new here, aren't you?" He sat the glass on the counter and leaned closer. "I can smell your innocence-*sssssss*..." His tongue slithered and licked my jaw.

I gasped and fell back from the counter onto the floor.

The music suddenly cut and everyone froze. Dancers and club employees alike craned their necks to look at me. I stood to my feet and glanced around. My arms shivered with goosebumps. I scanned the silent crowd for Kesi. I wanted to leave. Now.

Booker emerged from the crowd, pushing patrons out of the way like it was nothing. He didn't stop until he reached me. He gripped my arm.

"She's yours, Booker?" the bartender asked. His hands had changed. They were like claws, gripping the formica.

Booker turned towards the crowd of dancers. "She's mine," he announced.

The music started again and everyone returned to what they were doing. The dancers danced again. The bartender returned to making drinks, although I still felt his cat-like eyes on me.

Booker's hand never left my arm. I jerked myself free. "Where's Kesi?" I asked.

"Easy, luv." His finger twirled around one of my twists. "He got himself into a bit of trouble, innit. Don't worry, though. He bartered for your freedom. Cares for you, that one." He grinned again, looking me up and down. "I see the allure-"

"Take me to him." I shielded my chest, and my face felt on fire again, but not in a good way.

Booker laughed and stepped to the side. "This way."

I followed him through the club; this time, the dancers' costumes seemed a little more... real. I saw a woman with a tail shaking like she was possessed on the dance floor. A man with horns on his head also had hooves instead of feet. I'd never seen a costume look so real.

Booker took me to the steel door Kesi had disappeared through moments ago. Beside the door was a voluptuous woman leaning on a man who was sweating profusely. She was whispering in the man's ear, her long forked tongue licking the shell of his ear. Her eyes caught me and she smirked. She beckoned me with a curl of her finger, but Booker moved between us.

"Eyes forward, luv."

The steel door led to a flight of stairs and we went up. Another door opened to the brisk outside, behind the big building, and Kesi was there, shivering in the darkness. His eyes widened when he saw me.

"You said she'd be safe!" he yelled.

"What are you talking about?" I asked.

Booker raised his hand to silence us. "Don't you think it fair to explain to the little lady?"

Kesi fell quiet, his mouth fixed into frown.

"No?" Booker asked. "You're a worm, you know that? Lying and all-"

"Someone explain what the hell is going on," I said, focusing on Kesi. "What's he talking about?"

Kesi stepped closer to me, but his eyes were on the dirty ground. "I love you, Es. I always have. I never meant for any of this to happen-"

"Any of what? Spit it out." I folded my arms. I was getting sick of the creepiness. The mysticism. I just wanted answers. I wanted to go home.

"Maybe I can explain?" Booker asked. "The Underground isn't a normal club; I'm sure you've noticed. Blokes like him can come and get anything they want... for a price. Problem is, not many are willing to pay, innit?" He nodded his head toward Kesi who remained quiet and avoided my eye.

"What price? What are you talking about?"

"You gonna answer her?" Booker asked.

"I..." Kesi's eyes misted with tears when he finally looked at me. "I traded a piece of my soul for the app."

"You what?" I yelled.

"I needed it to do well, Es. I just lost Yasmine. Everything was changing. I didn't know what to do."

Booker stepped up to us and placed a hand on Kesi's shoulder. "Kesi's been a proper little gambler. Sowing terror into the hearts of men at night. Keeps him up, I'm sure. He's done his duties well... until tonight when he brought you here." He gripped Kesi's shoulder tightly and he winced in pain. "He just sold another piece of himself to keep you safe. Isn't that sweet, Esme? But there's one thing he should mention..."

My heart thumped in my chest, listening to Booker, but my eyes never left Kesi. He was holding back tears, and his voice wavered like water when he spoke.

"I belong to The Underground now. So we can't ever see each other again, Es."

"What?"

"There it is." Booker laughed and placed dark sunglasses on his face. "Isn't it better now that it's out in the open? Come now, I have nightmares to deliver." He snapped his fingers and a man with devil horns emerged from the darkness. I didn't know where he came from. He had my purse and handed it to me. "I'll escort you home, luv. Follow me." Booker turned on his heels. This was all happening so fast.

"Wait." I held onto Kesi's sleeve. "This is nuts. What do you mean we can't see each other again?"

"We just can't," Kesi said sadly.

The man with devil horns suddenly lifted me without effort. I kicked and screamed for him to put me down, but he wouldn't budge. I begged Kesi to help. For him to tell me what nightmare we both stumbled into, but he just stood there, wrapped in darkness, frightened to even look me in the face.

v. ebony

Why did I even come here?

My car keys are clenched in my hands, and I welcome the slight pain. My leg jitters as I look around the waiting room. It smells clean, like someone has just wiped down the seats with alcohol.

An audience laugh track sounds from the tv in the corner of the ceiling. It startles me. The receptionist who checked me in looks over at me and smiles. I don't smile back. I don't even want to be here.

I understand why I need to be, though. My older sister, Erica, so well-meaning, insisted that I saw help. *Professional* help. And if I didn't take this offer, she'd have to resort to more drastic measures. Like an institution. She told me as much.

And as much as my sister loves me, I know she's a woman of her word. So, that scares me.

I've been doing better. Much better than I was a couple of months ago when I had hit my ultimate low and was sent to the hospital. That was enough cause for Erica to pack up and move us far away from California. She settled on Germantown, a little neighborhood in Philadelphia.

It offers a quietness that feels like home with a busyness that I guess Erica thinks I need to function. Unfortunately for Erica, that means I'm close to the city and can find just about anyone to comfort me. And Erica is quick to pass judgment whenever I go out.

One night in particular, I remember Erica tagging along and she saw me making out with two guys at the same time. She pulled me away so fast, and we argued in the middle of the street. She threatened to take me home. In a fit of rage, she said she hated that I don't think more of myself. I responded that I'm a fuck up. I know that I am. Erica told me she just wanted me to be safe. And when I replied with a laugh and said, *I don't want to be safe. I want to die...* Well, that changed everything.

So here I am.

"Ebony Cross?"

I jolt at the sound of my name. A man enters the waiting room wearing thick black glasses that make me question whether he really needed them. He's tall, broad-shouldered, and wearing a dress shirt and slacks absolutely made for him. He extends his hand. "I'm Dr. Wu."

The raising of my eyebrow is strictly involuntary. He seems more like a model than a therapist, but I shake his hand anyway. I have red marks on my palm from clutching my keys and his eyes sweep over them, but he doesn't say anything.

"Ebony," I say and wipe my hands on my pant leg.

"Nice to meet you. This way." He goes through the doors and I follow him to a back office. There's a window overlooking Germantown Avenue, and I can hear cars driving over the cobblestone street below. It's so beautiful outside. I'd much rather be out there than stuck here.

His office is smoky from burning incense. It's burning from his desk, but there are also two incense holders on the coffee table. Two leather chairs face each other, and he takes a seat in one.

"Please," he says and I follow. "I'm sorry if the incense agitates you. I asked your sister if you had any aversions-"

I shake my head. "No, it's okay." It's strange. What was once a strong, nauseating smell starts to feel toasty, like I'm at a spa. "It's nice, actually."

"Good." Dr. Wu smiles. I've been afraid to look him in the face until now. I'm afraid he's going to read my thoughts. I'm afraid he will see how I stare at his large hands or how I wet my throat. But if he notices, he doesn't say anything about it. "I'm glad you came to see me."

I look at his face and study his eyes. I speak without filtering. "You look familiar."

He blinks. I can tell wha   's thinking within a second. *Do you think all Asians look the same?* I don't apologize or explain

82

though. His startled face only relaxes into a grim smile and he chuckles. "Perhaps I just have one of those faces?"

I nod. "Maybe."

He gets up from the chair and goes to a cart by his desk. It has an electric teapot and a lazy susan full of tea packets. "Can I offer you anything? Tea often calms my nerves."

"I'm not nervous," I say. I take this time to study his broad back. He glances over his shoulder and smiles. "I'll take tea."

He returns a moment later and the tea isn't too hot, so I sip it immediately. If only to take up time. He sighs as he settles back. "Ebony..." He exhales my name. "Ebony, Ebony, Ebony," he sings, patting the arm of the chair.

The tea freezes in my mouth. He relaxes into the leather chair and rolls his shoulders back. He takes a deep breath and grips the arms of the chair again. He exhales slowly and sits upright.

I swallow the tea. "Are you okay-"

He interrupts me. "What brings you in today?"

I set the tea in my lap. "I... um..." I'm at a loss for words. I've never done therapy before. Well, not like this.

When Erica and I moved to Germantown, I was still recovering from my accident. I didn't want to go out. Erica worked and provided for me, but when it had been weeks since I hadn't moved from the couch, she suggested I come with her to a group therapy session at some church. I definitely didn't want to go but having her there made it easier.

I had sat in the back, listening to everyone talk about their journey of grief. Erica had stood up to talk and when she spoke about her journey, I couldn't help but feel eyes on me, too. She talked about how hard things have been since our parents died. It's been suffocating to the point we had to move across the country to get away. Our older brother, Aaron, moved to Amsterdam with his wife and kids and left us behind. Erica said the pain of both losses was enough to leave California. She did it for herself, but also for her sister, at which point a room full of eyes centered on me. And they looked at the bandage wrapped over my arm.

I remember looking out into the room, at each of their faces and how the pity nearly suffocated me. Erica and I weren't the only ones struggling with grief. They all were, too. So why did they look like we were such unfortunate souls? It made me sick, all of them looking at us like that.

But I remember one man in particular. He had a scraggly beard, a black coat, and a hat that obscured most of his face. In a room full of sympathizers, his eyes were closed, inhaling deeply through his nose... and smiling.

When I told Ebony about it later, she told me not everyone at the sessions copes the same way and to just ignore the man. I don't know, if anything, that just made me want to clam up all the more. It made me never want to talk about my grief and snuff it out with anything. With anyone.

"Ebony?" Dr. Wu calls my name again with that familiar tune like I was a childhood friend.

"Well, my sister thought I'd do well with one-on-one counseling." I take another sip of tea. He waits until I'm finished to continue.

"Why does she think you need counseling?" He pushes his glasses back on his face. I want to clam up. I want to be silent, but the words tumble as easily as breathing.

"Because our parents died and Erica doesn't think sex or self-harm is a good coping mechanism."

His eyes trail down from my face to my right arm. It's covered with a long sleeve, but I still unconsciously pull it down. My face feels flushed suddenly. "I think this was a mistake."

I set the tea on the coffee table and don't make it past the chair when he calls my name again. Sharply. A controlled bark.

"Ebony."

I glance back at him, and he's gripping the arms of the chair again, breathing deeply. *"Sit. Down."* His voice has changed. It reaches into the pit of my stomach, and my feet move no matter how much I don't want them to. I turn back to the chair and sit perfectly erect. "Have something to drink," he says calmly.

I reach out for the cup of tea and try to fight it, but I drink it with one gulp. "Good, right?" he says. "Now, you're feeling a bit more relaxed."

I am. My body sinks into the leather chair. My head rests back and my fingers play on the arm of the chair. "I feel good."

"You do."

"What are you doing to me-"

"Tell me a time when you didn't feel good?" he asks. My eyes struggle to open, and I look over at him. He's hunched over, boring into my face, keenly interested in what I have to say. "How'd that happen to your arm?"

My brows scrunch together. "How'd you know about that?"

"Answer me."

My eyes shoot wider. "After my parents died, I tried to kill myself. I slit my arm open. Erica... she found me in the bathroom." My eyes well with tears at the memory.

Dr. Wu breathes in deeply. My chest sinks further into the chair and suddenly my heart hurts. Physically hurts. I want to cradle my chest in hopes of soothing it, but I can't even lift my arms. I look up to the ceiling as tears fall down my cheek. "Please, what's happening-"

"And how did your parents die?"

My eyes lower until I see him, still hunched over, leaning on his knees. His leg rocks. His eyes are closed like he's concentrating, or listening for something. Then he inhales again. He asks in an annoyed tone, eyes still screwed shut. "How did they die, Ebony?"

My eyes shut, and I bite my lip to stop myself from speaking. "In San Diego," I answer him. "We... we went on a walk at Sunset Cliffs."

I'm no longer in Dr. Wu's office when I open my eyes. I'm there, in San Diego. I'm walking ahead of my parents as we coast along the path. Erica had stayed behind to study, so it's just the three of us. Me and my parents. They're right there, talking. My mother's laughing at something my father said when I hear it. A gasp. Then a scream. It all happens within a second of turning around. They're gone.

A small collection of people hover by the cliff's edge looking down, many screaming. A few of them are already on the phone with a dispatcher. A scream tears through my throat and I run over. I don't know what I plan to do. Maybe reach through time to pull them back up? Or maybe go over the edge myself? But someone stops me. They hold me back from looking over the edge.

I blink and I'm back in Dr. Wu's office. My stomach feels queasy and cold when I see his mouth twist into a sickening smile, and he continues breathing deeply. When he opens his eyes, a small gasp escapes my mouth. His eyes are pools of black, void of white, and glinting.

"That's good," is all he says. "Very good." His voice reverberates around the room. He stands to his feet and heads over to his desk.

I swallow. "Please "

"And your brother, Aaron?" He pulls a long frayed rope from one of his drawers and takes his time coming over to me. He stops in front of my chair. "What happened to him?"

"How do you know about him-"

"Shh," he says softly. He wraps the rope around my neck, gives it slack, and waits. "Tell me about Aaron."

"He left us." The words tumble out my mouth, and I can't stop the tears from falling. "He left me after I got out of the hospital. He didn't want to be here. He didn't want to be around me."

Once again, when I blink, I'm whisked away from the office. I'm back in San Diego. I'm in my grief-stricken bedroom, piled with dirty clothes, dishes, and old takeout. Aaron is standing in the doorway, not daring to enter. He watches the lump on my bed, covered head to toe with blankets.

"You can't keep adding to the chaos, Ebony," he says. "You aren't the only one missing them."

I don't say a word. I pull the blankets further over my head.

"I can't be around this," he says before closing the door behind him. Erica tells me a day later that he's uprooting his family to live in Amsterdam.

I blink again and I'm back in Dr. Wu's office. Before me, I think I see Aaron standing where Dr. Wu had been. The rope starts to tighten on my neck and I gasp. My eyes trail up to see it's still Dr. Wu, still smiling, still telling me, "Good. You're doing good."

The rope constricts my throat. My fingers dance against the arms of the chair, grasping, clawing for control. My eyes grow heavy. My fingers begin to lose their fight. In the midst, I think of Erica. I think about how she's going to take the news. And as much as I wanted to die before, nothing compares to the guilt, the sudden vigor to live again. If only for her. I think about the group therapy session at the church. She stood tall in a room full of people, but I know Erica. She can't take another blow.

My fingers claw at the chair. My feet scuff against the carpet in feeble attempts to gain control, but Dr. Wu has an iron grip on the rope, tightening it more and more.

The telephone suddenly rings, and he jumps back. I cough and struggle to calm myself, gasping for breaths. His dark eyes turn back to normal, and he pats down his rumpled shirt. He takes a deep breath before answering the phone. "Dr. Wu."

His eyes widen and he looks over at me. "Yes, Miss Cross. I've seen her. She's here." His hand flexes into a fist and digs it into his desk, but he keeps his tone even. "Unfortunately, she's had another...episode."

My eyes widen. "Er...Erica." My voice is a whisper, and it hurts to speak. He turns toward the window where a dozen cars drive by below.

"Before coming to her appointment, she made another attempt on her life. She came to me very hysterical..." He waits a beat, and I can hear Erica crying on the other line.

My eyes cloud with tears and I shuffle my feet, move my fingers, but my voice cracks under the pressure. "No...Erica..."

"Right, she's told me she attempted before. She's alright now. I have a few recommended places for her to receive more help if you'd like. She... you'd like to speak with her?" Dr. Wu looks over his shoulder at me and then faces the window again. "Of course, she's still a bit shaken up. One second, please." He sets the receiver down and backs away from the window.

He removes his glasses and exhales loudly. He relaxes his broad shoulders. I hear a crack and his shoulders constrict inward, collapsing into a smaller frame. My palms sweat, and I watch in horror, as he tilts his head as if he's cracking his neck, but he's making it smaller, sinking it into his shoulders.

He shakes his legs, and they shrink, until he's my height. His body shifts, rounding out until I recognize a chest, hips, hands similar to my own. And then his face molds, mixing until it reaches the right-sized lips, the right-sized nose. But his eyes... his eyes stay the same.

He takes a deep breath and looks at me. My vision blurs. I can't make sense of it.

He picks up the receiver again. "Erica?" He parrots my voice and a cry bubbles from my lips.

"I'm okay now," he says into the phone. "I'm sorry... I want to follow Dr. Wu's recommendations. I need help, Erica." He starts crying.

"No, Erica..." My voice is still hoarse.

Dr. Wu says goodbye and hangs up. I watch myself come from the desk and stop in front of my chair. I feel like I'm floating. Like I'm barely tethered to earth as I stare into my own face, but everything is wrong. It's me, but so very off. My eyes... those aren't my eyes.

"Don't worry, Ebony. We're going to get you all the help you need. I promise." A finger caresses the side of my face until a grip seizes my throat. "You just need to *forget.*"

—

The past few days have been a blur. I've had dreams of smoke, leather chairs, and tea. I've had nightmares of rope and... dark, black eyes. But I remember. I *think* I remember seeing myself, talking to myself. I remember seeing Dr. Wu in his office. I remember telling him about my traumas and being afraid of dying...

I don't remember trying to take my own life again. But I have the red rings around my neck as a reminder. I'm really trying to remember, but the fact that I don't, scares me.

I agree to go to an institution called Belmont, under Dr. Wu's recommendations. I'm doing it for Erica. I want to get help. I need it. I... I don't want to feel like this anymore.

"You don't have to be here for long, you know." Erica's voice draws me back to the present. I've been sitting in the visitor's room, outlining the funky pattern on the table.

"I know."

Erica sighs and looks around. Patients sit at other tables, talking with family members. I can see it on Erica's face. She hates that I'm here. "You just gotta get better, you know?"

"I know." My finger still traces the table.

"Aaron is coming back," she says. "He'll come visit soon."

My eyes finally lift to see her. "What did you tell him?"

"I told him what happened. I told him that... you needed more help. That's all. I didn't say exactly why."

"I'm not even sure why." I glance around the room and my eyes settle on the orderly by the door. "So I must be crazy then."

"You're not crazy, Ebony."

"I don't even remember trying to kill myself."

"Maybe it was an out-of-body experience?" Erica suggests. The question is innocent enough, but it strikes something in me. Out-of-body...out-of-body...

Her hand rubs mine and pulls me from my thoughts again. I catch her gaze on my neck, and I unthinkingly reach to touch it. It stings when I touch the bruised area. Yeah, it really happened.

"I'm sorry that this happened, babe." Erica pats my arm. "But it's going to be okay, I promise."

I nod.

We talk a few moments before she has to leave and I only tear up when she does. Then I have to reassure her, echoing what she told me minutes before. "It's going to be okay, I promise."

It's my first day at Belmont and I'm assigned to a new therapist. I'm told he's a wonderful psychiatrist and he's been made aware of my apprehension about therapy, so he'll be gentle. Whatever that means.

Dread colors my face as I'm brought to a small office. Memories from the last time hang around every corner, but there's no incense. There's no cart of tea.

It was only days ago, but it feels like a lifetime. I feel so separated from it all that it almost feels like I dreamt the entire thing. Like I dreamt the suicide attempt and my frantic therapy session with Dr. Wu afterward and how I begged for his help.

I try to relax in the chair while waiting for the therapist to come. *It's going to be okay*, Erica's words echo in my mind. *It'll be okay.*

The door of the small office finally opens, and he comes in. I hear the door close behind him. He comes into view, shucking off his black coat and placing it over the padded chair across from me.

"So sorry I'm late," he says. He takes off his hat and sets it on his coat. I look at the clothing and then back at him. "Bad traffic on 76."

He's quiet as I study him. I take in his small shoulders and scrawny frame. I look over his black stubble and his thick glasses.

He exhales loudly and ends it with a smile.

I hug my knees as I sit further in the chair. "You look familiar." I blurt out.

And he chuckles, he laughs, making his mouth unusually wide. He rubs his hands on his thighs and squeezes them before letting go. He exhales again and looks me in the eyes.

"Oh, Ebony... Ebony, Ebony, Ebony," he sings my name. He leans forward in his chair. "What brings you in today?"

vi. corinne and travis

My great grandmama Cinna had been 117 years old when she finally joined the ancestors. She was buried in the backyard of our Wissahickon home in West Germantown, Philadelphia. I was eight years old at the time.

The local newspaper tried for weeks to interview her before she passed, scheming to gain a goldmine of experience of a world long gone, but Mama stopped them in their tracks every time they came knocking.

I remembered watching Mama, arm outstretched, calmly saying, "Not a step further." Her hair was twisted up, the longest pieces blowing in the crisp October wind, her apron stained with baked apple and cinnamon.

The reporter, an overly tanned woman with blonde hair, halted. "You're not welcome on these grounds," Mama said. "And you'll leave at once."

I watched in awe from our living room window, gently tugging on my newly twisted braids - a habit I developed whenever watching my mother cast. I observed how the woman spun on her heels, the cameraman following. They loaded up their van and pulled out of our driveway without a single glance back.

Mama Cinna passed away that night, but not before calling me into her room. She dismissed my entire family, including my mother and her seven sisters. She patted the spot beside her. She wiped my tears when I began to cry.

"Corinne," she said. "Even though some of us have the gift, we try not to prophesize. It always does more harm than good, but this is an exception." She wheezed, struggling to breathe. "I need you to know that in your adulthood, you're going to do something, something terrible, and it may affect you and the family." Her grip on my hand tightened, and her eyebrows furrowed. "You better not rest until you make it right."

Then she reached up and tapped my forehead three times.

And in the next breath, Mama Cinna was gone.

When I exited the room, my aunts and cousins surrounded the door. Auntie Sylvia pushed past me, calling for Mama Cinna. Everyone filed in after her, but my mama stood still. She glared at me, a contemplative look in her light eyes.

Seconds later, wails and emotional stomping erupted from Mama Cinna's room. The wood floor shook and moaned beneath my small feet, but Mama stayed put. The glass vase on the hallway table rattled, shifting closer and closer to the edge until it fell and shattered.

I jumped from the noise. The shattered vase, the cries coming from Mama Cinna's room, the house shaking. Pain ripped through the house and left me with so many feelings that I finally began crying.

"Mama?" My voice was so small, almost nonexistent.

"Did Mama Cinna say anything to you?" she asked. I thought about her question. Had Mama Cinna said anything to me? I couldn't remember.

"Did she touch your forehead at all?" she pressed.

I remembered that, so I nodded.

Mama's face softened. "It's okay, baby." She opened her arms to invite me in. I ran to her. I cried into her apron as she hugged me. "It's okay. Mama Cinna must've had a reason to make you forget," she said.

I never knew what Mama was referring to, but I'd been more than happy to put the night behind me.

Thirteen years later, I was meeting with my older cousin, Ksenia. We decided on Red Sun, a cafe near my house. When I stepped inside, the aroma of coffee and the sweet smell of vanilla and cinnamon warmed my mood and reminded me of my childhood.

The soft lighting in the cafe bounced off Ksenia's bald head. Her oversized gold hoops gleamed, and her smile beamed infectious energy that knocked the October chill from me. I adjusted my scarf as I went up to her.

"Hey, cuzzo!" she called, jumping up from the table. "Ooh, I love that red scarf especially against that brown skin, too, girl! You're glowing!" She pecked my cheek and slid a cup of coffee over. Ksenia knew how to make a girl feel good about herself. Loved that about her.

"So, not that I don't just *love* seeing you," I asked. "What's the urgency? I have a track meet in an hour."

Ksenia flashed completely white eyes before blinking, turning them back to their usual deep brown.

"Oh, I see. Is it good or bad?" I asked, cradling my coffee and taking a deep inhale.

She took a slow sip of her coffee, her gold bangles falling softly down her thin wrist. "Um, a bit of both. There's a guy," she sang with a smirk. "He's like, obsessing over you. I think he's someone you've seen or met, because I see our neighborhood. Maybe from work, or even a coffee shop. He's not your normal type, but girl, does he love him some you! I can just feel it."

Here we go again.

I rolled my eyes. "Is this real or does this have anything to do with Damien?"

She cut her eyes at me, and I immediately regretted the question. "You think I'd lie on my gift? Look, I'm sorry that he's gone. I'm not telling you to move on. Death is something that stains us. All I'm saying is someone else may want to make you happy. He doesn't need to be Damien's replacement."

I considered her advice although she didn't know the truth behind Damien's death. No one did.

"D'you have anything else? How am I going to know who he is?"

Ksenia rolled her eyes and sighed. "Just ungrateful. All I can say is look around next time. You may just catch him staring."

I sighed. "Alright, K. What's the bad?"

"You know how this goes. All I can say is that you'll find yourself in some trouble soon. Big trouble. And I'm sorry, Corinne," Ksenia said, covering my hand with hers. "I needn't remind you why Mama Cinna never allowed me to prophesize and why she didn't practice it herself. I can only give you so much without... *altering* things. But, I used Mama Cinna's protection prayer over this. Here." She handed me a twine bracelet from her other wrist. I took it, inspecting the gold flecks embedded in it. Ksenia had yet to be wrong. I gave her my wrist, and she tied the thin bracelet, knotting it.

"Cute," I chirped, ignoring the dread lingering in my stomach.

We talked about school, our grades, and guys. Before I knew it, I had to go. I stood to leave and she grabbed my arm.

"Make sure your tracker is on just in case I have to find your ass." We hugged goodbye as my mind raced. In case she had to find me? Was I in that much trouble?

I felt safer staying with Ksenia. I was tempted to skip work and school, *and* refrain from casting just to be with her, but I knew that she'd refuse. Changing one's routine was sometimes the precipitating action that brought about the exact event one's trying to prevent.

I got to my track meet and made an effort to look around as I stretched. The meet got underway and Ksenia's warning faded from my mind as I got more focused. I felt a trickle of rain drop on my hand and looked up. Oddly, I hadn't noticed the change in weather. The setting sun still glowed like an orb in the sky.

On my way inside to grab my gym bag and jacket, I felt eyes on me. Avoiding suspicion, I turned and waved goodbye to my teammates and met the piercing stare of a man sitting in the bleachers. I felt in my bones that this was the guy Ksenia was talking about. I definitely recognized him.

He suddenly stood, grabbed his belongings, and rushed out of the stands. He wore a blue shirt and black basketball shorts, and stood at about six feet, but it was hard to tell from so far away. Judging by his reaction, he was shy.

TRAVIS

She had a head full of tiny dark ringlets. They would bob as she ran laps around the outdoor track at school. Sometimes, the arms of her red frames would press a loose curl to the sides of her glistening face, slick with the dew of perspiration.

Her dark brown skin glowed under the pinkish-orange hue of the setting sun. I watched her from the bleachers, my laptop screen up so I didn't seem like a creep.

Corinne was utter perfection. Not in the way a snowflake is deemed symmetrically perfect. More in the way a canna lily, its asymmetrical petals and inconsistent hues, could be considered flawless. She was flawed in the most impeccable, lovely ways. When she ran, her lustrous hair bounced, full of life. Her eyes were focused and determined. She ran every day except Sundays, but I'd only visit the track when I'd finished my teacher's aide duties early.

On my walk home, I thought about seeing Corinne for the first time. It was about a month ago. I was jogging around the neighborhood and spotted her down a bricked alleyway. She glanced over both shoulders before ducking under a blue, tattered garage door.

Intrigued, I crouched behind the garbage bins at the alley entrance to see what she was doing. Within seconds she reappeared holding a bright yellow bird, gently petting its head. It tweeted and chirped in her hand. I remembered thinking how strange it was for someone to steal a bird. What could this beautiful girl possibly want with it?

Then I watched in shock as she twisted its neck until it ceased all movement and stuffed the bird into her backpack. She continued down the alley, completely normal. There had to be an explanation, I thought, as I finally stood to finish my jog. And yet, truthfully, the lack of a fitting rationale changed nothing about how I felt about her. If anything, I was more intrigued.

My family owned a large home on Bayton Street where I lived alone during the school year. My family resettled in Boston as a kid, but we'd frequent Philadelphia to visit family. When we weren't using the house, my mom rented it out. The quarter acre it sat on took lots of maintenance so a groundskeeper would visit weekly to work on the massive garden while I tended to the flower beds, at the behest of my mother. I didn't mind though. Watering, pruning, and repotting served as an escape. I found it all so very peaceful.

As I neared home, I felt the odd sensation of being followed.

I hurried once the safety of my front door was in view. A small black silhouette flashed in the corner of my eye. It peeked around a butterfly bush in my neighbor's front yard.

I stumbled to a stop and repeatedly blinked to clear my eyes. When I opened them again, the black silhouette was slightly larger. Squeezing the thin strap of my bag, I ran full throttle, taking my front steps by two up onto the rickety wooden porch.

I glanced back at the amorphous black shape floating towards me. Panicking, I fumbled with my key, but finally made it inside. I slammed the door shut and locked it.

Next, I remembered waking up on the floor. My back rested against the front door. The soft lace curtains surrounded me like a shroud.

I stood, my head spinning. My skin buzzed and burned. Nausea racked my stomach.

Was it flu season? Maybe I was coming down with something, I thought.

I spent twenty minutes soaking in the bath and felt somewhat better. As I sat in the hot water, my mind flitted to Corinne. I wondered where she was, what she was doing... what she was wearing. My back stiffened in protest of my own thoughts. I didn't want to pervert the image I had of her in my mind so I pushed her out.

When I stepped out, I stared at myself in the bathroom mirror. My eyes were bloodshot and red. My pupils were slightly dilated. I looked horrible and felt a deep exhaustion throughout my body.

Before settling in for the rest of the night, I decided to listen to Kendrick's new album and get some gardening done.

I stood over the vibrant red and yellow rose bushes that lined the fencing with my shears in hand. I stood motionless, as if in a trance until I noticed Corinne making her way up my block. When I realized she was headed for my fence, my heart dropped. I didn't readily acknowledge her presence and snipped a few flowers for the new vase my mother left for the entryway during her last visit.

"Hey there." She beamed. I stopped cutting and popped an earbud out.

"Oh, hi," I responded, casually.

"You go to my school, don't you? I've seen you around. You come to the track, and I noticed that you also live in my neighborhood," her eyes drifted past me, "in this gorgeous mansion no less. Are you a student?"

My hands trembled, so I shoved them into my pocket as I leaned on the fence separating us. "Yeah. I'm also a teacher's aide."

The urge to embrace her tugged at me. Suddenly, all I wanted to do was pull her into my arms and never let go. The intensity of my yearning frightened me. I had to get a hold of myself. My hands found my face and I rubbed aggressively. *Snap out of it, Travis.*

"I've seen you around, too, I think," I finally said.

When I looked up, she stood further away from me with a slightly puzzled expression. I wasn't convinced she completely believed me.

"Well, it's nice to finally meet." She held out her hand over the iron fence.

I hesitantly reached out, realized I still had my gardening glove on, and snatched it off. When I took her hand, it was soft. Her nails were manicured and painted black with a thin white spider web design. A violently intense urge washed over me again to take her into my arms. I didn't want to let go of her hand. I didn't want to let *her* go. There was an internal fight to release her hand. I came to my senses and released her from my grip.

"The name's Corinne," she said.

"Nice to finally meet you, Corinne. I'm Travis." She shifted her body, positioning herself away from me. I didn't want her to go yet, but then she smiled and asked a question.

"Are you going to that Halloween party?"

"Uh, actually no. I'm not a huge fan of Halloween. I see it's your favorite though," I said, pointing to her fingernails. She nodded in agreement. "Unfortunately, I have a shit ton of work to do, so I'll be too busy to go."

"Well, that's too bad. I would've loved to see you there," she said, walking off, "I'll see you around, Travis." I watched her go, like water slipping through my fingers. My eyes rested on her back, her small shorts hugging her body. She finally turned onto Germantown Ave and out of sight.

I missed her already but felt I'd be seeing her sooner than I thought.

CORINNE

The night of the Halloween party, I stood in the mirror questioning whether I wanted to attend. Grief hit me like a ton of bricks this afternoon and stole any excitement I had about going. It loomed over me like a dark cloud. I blamed myself for Damien no longer being here and the guilt choked me at random moments.

I almost didn't recognize my red, puffy eyes staring back at me. I still couldn't believe he was gone, so young and full of life.

Several months ago, through the crack of my bathroom door, Damien caught me practicing a simple healing spell Ksenia taught me. I thought it'd be the end of us. Even though I knew it was one of the biggest offenses against my family, I told him the truth about who I was. *What* I was.

I should have come clean to my family, but I loved Damien.

The night Damien died, I stood dealing with the consequences of my actions.

We were sitting on the Philadelphia Art Museum steps sharing a basket of french fries and ketchup. Damien took the wave brush from his pocket and ran it across the top of his head. The moon was full, casting a beautiful white glow on the trees and buildings around us. We'd been arguing, and I grew tired of saying the same thing over and over.

My stance hadn't changed over the past few weeks since he found out my secret. Damien wanted me to spellbind his professor, even after I'd explained that certain spells require my elders' input or were best done with two people. I was still learning the craft from Ksenia who was a master incantation writer. I was only *moderately* skilled at it.

Due to his failing grade in Psych class, he was in danger of sitting out for the season again and losing his scholarship so he was desperate. I looked into his pleading, deep brown eyes and dropped my shoulders in defeat.

I spellbound his professor that night. Or so I thought.

I waited until we were alone on the museum steps. Since it wasn't a particularly involved spell, I decided to freestyle the incantation. According to my studies, the worst that could happen was for it not to work.

Words flowed out of my mouth like honey and it was invigorating. Damien looked on, his eyes wide with awe.

"Wow, babe," he muttered, "you're looking real sexy right now." He bit his lip, rubbing his hands together.

The wind blew dead leaves all around us and Damien shielded his eyes. At the last minute, I removed a hair from Damien's brush to permanently bind him to the spell, so there was never another threat to his scholarship. It was a riskier addition, but it would've made the spell stronger.

The wind died down, and I giddily turned to face him once the last word was spoken. "It's done, babe."

The smile faded from my face.

When I looked over at Damien, he was slumped to the side, almost falling down the stone steps of the museum. I reached over and shook him by the shoulders.

"Damien!" I screamed. A woman walking by with her dog ran up to us and called an ambulance.

Damien was taken away to the hospital, and I didn't see him again until his funeral.

When I reviewed my incantation, I realized that my pompous decision to make the spell stronger and bind Damien was actually the fatal error. He paid the ultimate price. Luckily, the professor came out unharmed.

Overcome with grief, I tried redoing the spell. I was even desperate enough to secretly attempt necromancy, and I wasn't surprised that it didn't work. I didn't have the skill it took. It was a huge offense to even attempt and if Mama ever found out, she'd skin me alive. Fortunately, nothing I tried bore any fruit.

My phone buzzed, pulling me from my thoughts. It was Ksenia asking if I was still meeting her to walk to the party. I looked at myself one last time, shoved my hair into a black witches hat, and cleaned up my makeup. I didn't have it in me to put much effort into my look tonight, so I chose the obvious. I grabbed my broom and walked out the front door.

The party was packed. Soon after arriving, Ksenia and I split up. She was meeting a special someone here. We agreed to regroup in about two hours.

I sat down on a plush brown couch with two other people, bobbing my head to Rihanna's voice, when my eyes fell on Travis. He stood in the doorway between the kitchen and living room. He wore a varsity jacket as his costume. His brown eyes glinted, and he gave a boyish smile. He put his hand up near his face and gave a small wave using just his fingers. It was something Damien used to do. Weird, but I couldn't help but smile. I was surprised and a little relieved to see him. I didn't know anyone here.

He made his way over, and there was something different about him as he walked. Maybe whatever was in his solo cup was to blame, but he had a familiar swagger about him, an attractiveness and gravitational pull I didn't feel when we met earlier. He came up to me with a sly smile, and I flirtatiously returned the gesture.

"Hey, babe," he said in a deep tone. The smile instantly faded from my lips. Travis stood there bobbing his head and eyeing me up and down. "You're looking real damn good tonight."

I hopped up and grabbed him by the arm, pulling him hard and fast and was met with no resistance.

I led us outside to the porch where people were dancing, drinking, and making out in full display. It was too crowded, so I peeked alongside the house and saw a narrow pathway that led to the backyard. Still pulling Travis' sleeve, I followed the broken, chipped path that opened to a large, empty yard. I whipped around to face him.

Before I could say anything, Travis spoke. "He wants to know why you killed that bird."

It caught me off guard.

Travis nonchalantly rocked his shoulder back and forth to the music blaring from inside the house, as if he'd just commented about the weather. He sipped from his cup.

"What are you talking about?"

Travis looked away. I thought about how I could go about this and get the answers I needed without revealing too much about myself, in case I was wrong.

He looked at me softly and touched my hand. "He saw you that day, babe. You went under that garage door, rescued that bird, and snapped its neck like it was nothing."

"Who saw me?"

He took another sip. His cavalier nature was driving me insane. I slapped the cup out of his hand.

"Who are you?" I finally asked. Travis stopped all movement and eyed me intently as if giving the question real thought.

A dark figure emerged from the pathway, and as it got closer, I saw that it was Ksenia. "Get away from him, Corinne!" she yelled and backed up immediately. I joined her side. "That's not Travis."

"Yeah, I know." I watched the way Travis was looking at me. It felt so different. It felt... familiar. "I think it's Damien."

Ksenia snapped her head towards me. "What the *hell* did you do, Corinne?" I opened my mouth, but she talked over me. "Are you fucking kidding me? You attempted necromancy?" I winced from the anger in her voice.

"I didn't think it worked." My voice came out small.

"You think?"

"I didn't mean for this to happen-"

As we argued, Travis slowly began changing. His bones cracked as he fell to the ground with a sickening thump. The look of anguish on his face broke my heart. His lips stretched in both directions, splitting the corners of his mouth and specks of blood pooled down his chin. Travis reached out for help, and I was tempted to take his hand if it weren't for Ksenia pulling me back by the shoulder.

"Help me," she ordered, reaching out for my hand. We held hands, reciting Mama Cinna's protection spell in hushed tones.

In a matter of seconds, Travis's body stopped contorting and lay still on the grass. From his back, something small and black permeated through his jacket. It transformed into a black puff of smoke floating up and away blending into the night sky.

Ksenia gripped my hand, leading us away from the party.

TRAVIS

I woke up with a splitting headache. I thought taking a nap would make me feel better, but I just feel like hell. I reached up to touch the bandages on my face and winced.

Since coming home from the hospital, bits and pieces from the last twenty-four hours played in my mind. I remembered coming home from the track meet. And then... that damn demon or whatever, attacked me. I stood up and groaned. My joints were on fire, but I pushed through it and got dressed in the clothes closest to me.

While I was being held hostage by that *thing,* he took my interest in Corinne and twisted it into some sort of perversion. It felt like an overwhelming obsession. She was all I thought about. I tried to fight back, and it nearly killed me. The voice in my head repeated a name. Another victim?

I went to the bathroom to clean up my face, but when I saw my reflection in the mirror, a sickening feeling bubbled up in my stomach.

The name suddenly came to mind. Coach Levi. Corinne's coach.

I stood before the sink, staring at myself and considered my options. I could stay home, stay safe, and be relieved that I was free from the prison I was locked in.

On the other hand, I could think about how it felt to share a space with an unearthly being, to be in anguish and struggle to control all your thoughts, feelings, and actions. If Coach Levi was the next target, no one would even know.

Dread wrapped itself around my neck and I could barely breathe. I took a deep breath and finalized my decision as I exhaled. I grabbed my phone and called my professor to see if he knew how I could reach Coach Levi.

CORINNE

I messed up. I messed up big time. My right hand blindly stumbled across the 300-year-old table, knocking over open bottles of elixirs and ingredients.

"Shoot!"

I dropped the recipe book and scrambled to salvage what was left of my concoction. The oven beeped, letting me know it reached my desired temperature and was ready to receive whatever I planned to put inside. If it only knew.

Sweat trickled down my forehead and landed in the pie filling. I paused, feeling a cool gust of air blow across the back of my neck. My shoulders involuntarily rose. I glanced behind me and no one was there.

"Ok, Corinne," I blew out. "You can do this."

Smoothing out my apron, I added the last few ingredients: cinnamon, nutmeg, three feathers from a trapped bird, a few of my fingernail clippings, and my last fire poppy. I mixed it all up, poured the filling into the crust, and slid the pie into the oven. I closed the oven door and sighed, finally unlocking the warning I received many years ago. "Mama Cinna, I promise I'm gonna make this right."

Ksenia burst through the french doors of the cottage. Our family owned the main house and we had this cottage built on the grounds a few years back. No one really used it anymore to bake spells and cast. It was the perfect place for us to fix my mistake in solitude.

"Okay," she said in a huff like she'd been running. "I had to go all the way to North Philly to get this." She slammed down a tattered brown book on the table. It didn't have a title, but I knew what it was. It was Mama Cinna's book of spells. "Don't tell my mama I took it."

I shook my head. I wouldn't dare.

"So, I did some research. I learned that the black entity we saw last night was a piece of Damien. I don't think you finished the necromancy spell or did it correctly. So instead of his soul returning to his body, poor Travis got possessed. How's he doing?"

"I did a simple spell to see into his home. He was released early this morning from the hospital. He may still be sleeping, so I'm not yet sure what he remembers. The pie is in the oven. He won't remember the last week or so."

Ksenia nodded approvingly.

I felt so bad for Travis. He was an innocent bystander, a casualty of my mistakes.

"I'm not sure how the guy even survived what happened," Ksenia said. "From what I read, most people don't. It's good we were there to cast Mama Cinna's protection spell over him." She walked over to the oven and peeked inside at the pie. "Once we give this to him, we need to find Damien and send him back."

"Right."

Ksenia sat in an old wooden chair in the corner of the room. "I'll try to find him in the meantime. Usually my visions come involuntarily, but I'm going to have to intentionally see where his spirit's hiding and it's dangerous. It's important you don't touch me unless my breathing rate drops too low. You have your timer up?"

I nodded, phone in hand.

Her eyes swiftly turned their milky white hue and her head dropped back like a rag doll. Her shoulders slightly jerked, and her boots slid back and forth across the dusty hardwood floor. I counted eight breaths per minute.

She breathed slowly and deeply until it looked like she was barely breathing. She finally closed her eyes, sinking into a place I'd never been.

"Don't read the incantation until I'm done," she said calmly.

I nodded. Ksenia was impeccable at writing incantations. I saw the paper underneath the cover of Mama Cinna's book. I was tempted to look over what she wrote, but decided to trust Ksenia's warning.

A light tap on the door about ten minutes later made me jump. I looked over at Ksenia and she wasn't done. I didn't know who it could be, but I was certain no one was home.

"Come on, K, hurry up," I whispered.

"Corinne, is that you?" a voice called.

I ran over to Ksenia and gently tapped her. "Ksenia, Ksenia wake up. It's my mom. Wake up!"

Ksenia's head raised and her eyes shot open. They were still white and devoid of color. Her mouth opened like she was about to screech, but she snapped it shut. She spoke in a quiet monotone.

"The boy's taken residence inside your track coach," she said, in a low, deep foreign voice. I stepped back.

"Ksenia?" I whispered urgently, "Is that you?"

"Since we were disturbed, she will need a full day's rest before she awakens." Ksenia's head limply dropped back again.

Mama called out for me and knocked harder.

I struggled to drag Ksenia's chair to the closet to hide her and sprinted to the door before Mama could burst through.

I opened the door and smiled. I smoothed down my apron, which used to belong to her. Mama stared at me, holding a bouquet of flowers in her hand.

"What are you doing back here?"

I shrugged. "Just baking."

"Baking? Or *baking?*" She raised her brow.

I laughed. "Regular ol' baking, Mama."

She eyed me then looked past my shoulder to see inside. "Hm," she hummed, handing me the flowers. "These are for you."

"Oh, thanks, Mama," I grinned.

"They're not from me. They were dropped off for you." She lifted the card attached to the bouquet. "Levi? Your coach, Levi?"

I blinked and I remembered what Ksenia said. *The boy's taken residence in your track coach.* I thought of a lie. "Oh, yeah. He sent out flowers to all the girls as a thank you."

"Oh." She handed me the flowers. "Have you seen Ksenia? Auntie Sylvia is looking for her, and she is not too thrilled." My heart dropped.

I lied again. "She went out for coffee, I think."

Mama eyed me incredulously, but surprisingly, didn't press the issue. She left without a word, walking back towards the house.

A huge sigh rolled off my shoulders. I closed the door and tossed the flowers on the table. Ksenia was still out of commission, sleeping in the chair by the closet. I was on my own. Travis would have to wait.

I grabbed the incantation Ksenia wrote. I checked on her, ensuring she was still breathing before heading out to take care of this issue.

Coach Levi had driven our team to many races in the past and oftentimes, we had to meet up at his house, so I knew where he lived. He didn't have a wife or children, so doing this was a bit easier which led me to the conclusion that Damien must've chosen him purposely.

I pulled up to his Chestnut Hill home, surrounded by large trees. His white Volvo station wagon was parked in the driveway.

I didn't have a plan, but it didn't stop me from trying the front door. It was open. I walked into the enclosed porch and the smell from the house nearly knocked me out. It was downright putrid; it was the unmistakable iron-like smell of blood and decaying flesh. I stifled the vomit that threatened to burn its way up my throat.

I ventured into his living room, my shirt hiked over my nose, but it did nothing to ward off the smell. "Damien?" I called into the darkness. All the lights were off, the shades in the living and dining room drawn. Twilight still managed to bleed through the blinds, casting the downstairs in strips of fading light.

I slowly moved into the kitchen, Ksenia's incantation firmly in hand. As I stepped into the kitchen, the smell of death became unbearable, and I gagged. I turned to step back out, but slipped on something wet on the tiled floor.

Dark, red blood pooled at my feet. I followed the trickling trail to a furry lump heaped by the counter. It was shrouded in darkness, but I could see its pointy ears, its whiskers dripping with blood. Its body had been slashed open, and I recoiled at the sight of its exposed heart, tripping over myself until I ran back to the living room.

I gulped the rancid air. Fear rattled my bones. I wished Ksenia were beside me. I wished I had her help.

The sound of a lamp's chain being tugged startled me, and I looked back into the corner of the living room. Coach Levi sat in an armchair, partially illuminated by the lamp. Blood coated his mouth and chin, and he smiled.

"Sorry for the mess," he said. His legs were crossed at the ankles. The calmness of his posture brought Damien to mind. And seeing him like this, licking the blood off his fingers was horribly disorienting. Coach Levi's blonde hair was disheveled and dirty. His white shirt was soaked with blood and glistened under the dim lamp. His piercing blue eyes were bloodshot and dilated. The image, the knowledge that I did this to him, brought me to tears.

"I'm so sorry, Coach Levi. Please forgive me," I pleaded.

His mouth opened wide with broken pitched laughter.

"Babe, he ain't here. It's just you and me. Like it will always be. Your coach was easier to take. I'm not sure why. Maybe because he has a major flaw." He finished licking the blood off his fingers and wiped them on his pants. "All I can say is, he really likes coaching the girls team." He shook his head. "Sick mind, this one. I wish I could have stayed in that other one. Travis, I think his name was? Man, did he fight me. He really liked you, Corinne. But it's not like the love I have for you, of course."

My fingers shook as I held up Ksenia's incantation. I couldn't stand to hear him talk anymore.

117

Damien sat up straight and laughed. "I know you're not serious. You killed me with your faulty ass spellcasting, failed to bring me back, and while I suffered in pain, being stuck in the ground for God knows how long, you just went on with your life. Even entertaining new guys? No, Corinne." He laughed again. "You think I'll allow you to put me back?" He stood to his feet. "The thing is babe, if *I* go, you're coming with me."

He lunged forward and tackled me. The air knocked out of me when my back hit the floor. Ksenia's incantation floated away from my hand, and I reached out to grab it.

We rolled on the ground, clawing at each other, and desperately trying to get the incantation. Damien pressed his body over me as he tried to reach it first. I was being crushed under Coach Levi's weight. He was squeezing the air from my lungs. I was suffocating.

He was inches from the incantation when the front door flew open.

Coach Levi's body flew off of me, and I could see that it was Travis. His face was bandaged, but he frowned as he held Coach Levi back, pinning his arms behind his head.

I grabbed Ksenia's incantation and stood to my feet. I glanced back and forth between Travis and the paper in my hand. Why the hell was he even here?

"Read it!" Travis demanded. He was struggling to stay in control. "Read the damn paper!"

I broke out of my daze and held up the incantation.

"Damien, your life was wronged,
you've been falsely rebirthed,
your spirit's a perversion here,
now return to the Earth."

Coach Levi suddenly went limp in Travis' hold. His head snapped up and Travis shouted, dropping him to the floor.

Coach Levi fell like a sack of bones. He slowly turned his head, his eyes fixed on me. His bloody mouth twisted in a smile, but he spoke with venom. "You're killing me twice, Corinne."

My throat ached and tears brimmed in my eyes. I held up the incantation and repeated it one last time, my heart breaking with every word.

Coach Levi's body went still. Black smoke permeated from his skin, swirling until it convened into a single puff. It floated upwards, disappearing before it ever reached the ceiling.

Travis fell back, hitting his head on the wall. "Travis!" I ran to him. I held him in my arms as his eyes involuntarily closed.

TRAVIS

I woke up in my bed again. This time, Corinne sat at my side holding a piece of pie with a dollop of whip cream.

"So," she said with a half smile.

I opened my eyes wider and felt more awake than I had in a long time. I tried to smile, but it hurt because of the stitches on the corners of my mouth.

Her hand touched my arm. "Travis, I cannot begin to explain how sorry I am. Also, I can't express my gratitude for coming to Coach Levi's house and helping me. I don't think I would've survived if you hadn't come."

"For you, anytime." My head swam when I sat up. "Everything feels hazy. Like I lost time."

She grabbed my hand and softly rubbed her fingers across my knuckles. My heart jumped at her touch. I knew I should be alarmed after everything that happened and probably stay far away from her. But I liked her, and wanted nothing more than to be near her.

"Can I take you out for a drink, coffee maybe?" I asked.

Corinne looked genuinely surprised, but smiled. She pushed her red frames up on her face. "I think I would've liked that." Her smile turned sad when she held up the pie. She forked a small sliver of pie and brought it to my mouth. Cautious of my stitches, I opened my mouth and took a bite.

vii. mallorie

The flash from the camera makes me see stars. I rub my eyes as I thank the woman who agreed to take our picture.

"Happy Halloween!" she calls as she disappears back into the sea of trick-or-treaters flooding Germantown Avenue.

"I'm dizzy," Lori comments. I look down at my twin sisters blinking, trying to chase away the white spots from the flash.

"I'm dizzy, too." Laura laughs and they take each other's hand and twirl around on the sidewalk. They're wearing identical princess gowns—Lori is in pale blue, Laura is in soft pink, and they both have translucent fairy wings stitched to their backs. They continue to laugh and twirl in place, almost bumping into other trick-or-treaters.

"Okay, girls, enough," Mom says and corrals them out of the way.

We move along, following a small group to the next house. I snap a picture of Lori and Laura as they step up to the porch.

"I've filled my quota, I think," I say. Mom rolls her eyes, but then her attention is back on the girls, watching how they conduct themselves on a stranger's porch.

"The night's barely started." She crosses her arms and looks at me. "I thought you'd like to take pictures tonight, Miss Photographer."

I roll the disposable camera in my hand, overanalyzing it. "I would've brought an *actual* camera."

"That *is* an actual camera." Mom laughs, throwing an arm over my shoulder and squeezing me. "New York has crowded your mind. You forget your roots."

I freeze in her embrace and stare at the sidewalk. "I should have stayed at school."

She releases me and sighs. She chews her cheek, a tick she does when thinking hard about something. "Have you made any friends yet at Syracuse?" she asks softly, like I might explode if she isn't careful.

"No. Just me. . . and my roommate. We don't really talk much. Apparently, she doesn't like people like me."

"What? Black people?" Mom's hackles raise, as if she would fight my roommate right then and there.

It brings a smile to my face, but I shake my head. "No, not Black people."

Understanding falls over her face and the fight leaves her body. "Oh," she says. And admittedly, it hurts a little that she isn't willing to fight anymore. "How does she know?"

I shrug. "She asked. I told her."

"Oh, Mallorie."

Our attention turns to Lori and Laura coming back. They're hype because that house decided to give out king-sized candy bars—which my mom takes from them and says they'll get it later. We journey to the next house, and Mom and I hang back again to watch.

"You can't go around telling people that," Mom says, continuing our conversation. "Everyone isn't as. . . accepting."

"You're accepting. Michael *was* accepting. That's all I care about."

I feel her eyes on me, and I choose to ignore them. Instead, I roll the camera and blind her with the flash.

"Ow, Mallorie!"

"What?" I laugh. "I thought you wanted me to take pictures tonight."

She rubs her eyes and pushes me. "You're an asshole."

"You raised me."

We continue through the neighborhood, and I take in my home. I've only been at Syracuse for a few weeks, but coming back here, I feel like I've grown years older. To be fair, I never wanted to go as far as New York for college, but after the hell I went through senior year - being outed at school *and* my brother dying in a car accident - I wanted to get as far away as possible.

It helps that I've decided to come back on Halloween, when people are dressed up and hiding their true selves. And I, in turn, don't have to recognize anyone from my past. I can hide behind this cheap camera and underneath Michael's Space Jam hat and revel in the beauty of Germantown without exposing myself.

And Germantown is a thing of beauty tonight. It's flooded with lights, laughter, and shuffling feet. Houses are decorated with illuminated skeletons and jack-o-lanterns. Wind sweeps through the streets, rustling the dead leaves. It's a bit chilly, but I have my uncle's old flannel to keep me warm.

Distant screams echo down the street followed by what I can only assume is mechanical ghoulish laughter. Laura squeezes my hand, and I look down at her. She has her own little flashlight. She shines it in the direction of the screams.

"It's okay," I say, smiling at her big innocent eyes looking up at me. "It's just a prank."

"What's a prank?" she asks.

"I...um." Unsure how to explain, I search for Mom to help. She and Lori are ahead of us, turning down a driveway toward a huge house decked out with ghosts hanging from the front yard trees.

"It's just a joke. And since it's Halloween, it can be a little scary, but that's all it is. It's just a joke," I say, forcing a smile.

Laura scrunches up her little nose. "It sounds mean."

"Well, that's the other part of Halloween. *Trick* or treating."

"Did Michael like trick-or-treating?" she asks and the question seizes my heart.

I rub the back of her hand with my thumb. "He did. He was a bit of an asshole, so he liked the tricking part more." I laugh and Laura chuckles with me.

As the night goes on, Mom accompanies the twins to each house and I stay back, snapping pictures from afar. Lori beams for a picture as she skips down the driveway, and trips from her long dress, but I catch her before she falls. She gives me a huge jawbreaker the size of my palm as a thank you. I'm tempted to suck on it as we walk, but I decide against it and stuff the jawbreaker in my pocket. The candy weighs heavy against my leg as we journey to the next house.

Across the street, I notice a group of kids. They're rowdy, hype, and dressed in scary costumes. They're walking in the opposite direction sporting fake blood and sharp teeth, pushing each other and laughing. There are a lot of them. I count seven kids altogether, but what makes me stop is the tallest of the group. He doesn't have a body frame that screams pre-adolescence like the rest.

He's wearing a goalie mask. I'm not sure if he's trying to look like Jason from *Friday the 13th*; his mask is different. It's dirty and charred like it'd been set on fire. And he's wearing a blue stained jumpsuit. Actually, the more I look at it, the cooler and scarier it seems.

Friday the 13th was one of Michael's favorite movies. I hope I'm not going to be reminded of him all night. But I do like this kid's costume.

Without thinking, I take a picture. His head snaps over at the sound of the clicker, and my heart drops. I'm not sure how he heard it across a busy street, but he stops and looks directly at me. The kids in front keep walking without him.

His body turns to face me, and he just stands there. The cut-out holes where his eyes should be feel like they're burning me. My mouth goes dry. I'm not sure what to do. Do I mutter an apology? Do I tell him I'll rip up the picture once the film is developed?

But then again, he doesn't even seem angry. His shoulders bounce like he's chuckling, and he gives me a little wave. I don't wave back.

A man emerges behind him, stepping out from the shadowy trees lining the street. He places a glistening white hand on the boy's shoulder. He, too, is wearing a goalie mask. It's charred and a piece is broken off the top. Like the boy, he's wearing a blue jumpsuit, but the front is covered with... dark red... What is that? Is it paint? Whatever it is, it glistens underneath the moonlight.

The man is very, *very* tall, like he's on stilts, so when the boy looks up at him, he nearly breaks his neck. The boy taps the larger man's hand still resting on his shoulder. The man walks off moving in slow motion. His white hands swing back and forth as he strides down the street, taking large steps.

The boy stands there a moment longer, still staring at me. Then he finally turns around and follows the man.

"Ready for the next house?"

"Shit." I jump and drop the camera.

Mom sucks her teeth. "Your mouth, Mallorie."

"Sorry," I say and pick up the camera. I glance down the street. "I saw something freaky."

Mom shrugs. "Well, it *is* Halloween. The camera okay?"

I look it over and load the clicker. Lori and Laura stand behind Mom arguing about what candy they want, and I take a picture.

"Hey!" they yell in unison when the flash blinds them.

"Yep," I laugh. "Still works."

As the night wears on, I gravitate towards Lori's bucket and take out a king-sized KitKat. Thankfully, she's too preoccupied with going to the next house to notice. I hang back again as they reach the porch.

A gaggle of laughs causes me to look towards the end of the block. The chocolate freezes in my mouth.

It's three boys who graduated with me from high school last year. They're walking down the street, all dressed in jeans and sneakers. Except for the only girl walking in front. Courtney Lake. She's wearing a yellow dress and kitten heels, standing out against the colorless crowd. Her brown braids are pulled into a high ponytail. Her beauty makes me sick. She's wearing a jean jacket that's way too big, with Class of '96 stitched onto the breast pocket. I recognize it from selling class jackets with student council.

Her boyfriend, Hugo, walks beside her, hugging her waist. He was always an asshole in our math class. He's walking so close to Courtney that they *have* to be recycling air.

I pull my hat down and step to the edge of the sidewalk. I even hold my breath for whatever reason.

"Mallorie Jones?" Courtney sings.

"Mala-*freak?*" Hugo says. They come to a stop.

Courtney comes out from her small group, but Hugo isn't but two steps behind her.

"I thought it was you under that hat." She steps closer and my foot slips off the sidewalk, but she catches me. She looks at the Kitkat in my hand. "How cute, you're still trick-or-treating."

"I'm not." I feel stupid for defending myself and even stupider when I feel four pairs of eyes look at the kingsized candy bar in my hand.

"Come on, Court," Hugo says and pulls on Courtney's wrist.

"You know," Courtney jerks her hand away. "If you aren't trick-or-treating, you could hang with us."

A collection of groans roll behind her, and I selectively choose to ignore it.

"I wouldn't want to cramp your style-"

"Come on, Mallorie," Courtney whines, as if I were Hugo who needed to hear just the right pitch to fold.

I analyze her face. Did she choose to forget why we stopped being friends? Does she not care anymore? Or more unlikely, does she miss me?

But even if she does, this feels like a trick. "I don't think it's a good idea-"

"For old times, Mal," Courtney says, without puppy eyes, without teasing. She looks into my eyes like she wants to say something else, but before I can ask, Mom and the twins come back.

Laura seizes my leg, squealing over how much she loves Halloween, and Lori is already stuffing her face with rock candy.

"Courtney Lake," Mom greets her. "I haven't seen you in ages. How's your mother?"

Courtney smiles stiffly. "She's good, Miss Jones. It's great to see you. How are you holding up?"

I know the look that flashes over Mom's face. The look that says, *how do I even begin to explain the process of losing my only son, raising two rowdy girls, and putting a daughter through college?*

In the end, Mom only smiles. "We're doing well."

"Well, you look great." Courtney grins, and Mom laughs awkwardly.

"Oh, thank you," she says, then she nudges my arm. "Ready to go?"

I look between her and Courtney. Courtney's back faces the guys, and I think I understand. She's hanging out with a group of college boys on Halloween. Does she just want a familiar face in her circle? She all but confirms it when she looks into my eyes. *"Please,"* she mouths.

Something twists in my chest at her plea. Suddenly, all I can think about is the girl who was my best friend from middle school to twelfth grade. Despite what happened between us, I can't turn away from her. I can't tell her no.

I tell my mom that I will be hanging out with her for the rest of the night, and she agrees that it'll be good for me.

"Why'd the hell you do that?" one of Hugo's friends asks Courtney when I join them on the corner.

"Look, it's going to be fun." Courtney wraps an arm around my shoulders. It's the most contact we've had since junior year. "I have a special treat for us tonight."

Turns out, the special treat that Courtney has planned is getting wasted at the park on Germantown Avenue. She uses a fake ID to buy three six-packs from the corner store.

Hugo kisses her squarely on the mouth for her contribution to the night. When he pulls away from her, I notice his class of '96 ring glints on his middle finger. I want to groan. This guy is stuck in high school.

He sees me staring and frowns. "What are you looking at, freak?"

Courtney touches his chest to calm him down. She hands him a beer and tells him to shut up.

I don't say a word. I don't even drink. I sit beneath a tree, hands in my pockets, as they break into the beer.

"What's that camera for?" One of Hugo's friends comes to me a moment later.

I look at the camera in my lap and shrug. "Pictures."

"No duh, smart ass," Hugo says. He shakes his head. "Look, Court isn't the only one with something fun tonight." He digs into his backpack and pulls out rolls of toilet paper. His friends giggle like schoolboys. They push each other in excitement as they head deeper into the park. I sit in the grass and watch them toss the toilet paper back and forth, stringing it on the trees.

A beer floats in my face, and I look up to see Courtney extending it towards me. I take it, but I don't open it. She plops down beside me.

"Why did you ask me to come here?"

She sighs. "I feel... bad."

I chuckle and look at the entrance of the park. The streets have gotten quieter. Trick-or-treaters have returned home. Houses have turned out their porch lights. Now, cars roam by every few minutes, leaving us in the dark. In the quiet.

"You feel bad," I repeat. Suddenly, the beer looks good, and I take my first sip. "Why?"

"You know why." Her eyes don't leave my face. "I wish our senior year was different."

"Well, actually that wasn't your fault. It was mine for telling you how I felt. That bitch, Sabrina, is the one who told everyone." I take another sip. "But then again after Michael died, you stopped talking to me-"

131

"I know." Her hand touches my knee. Her brown eyes look darker under the shadows of the tree. "And I'm so sorry, Mal. I really am."

I study her face a moment longer before drinking again. We sit in comfortable silence until I ask her about college. She tells me about Cornell. I tell her about Syracuse. She asks about my mom and tells me how envious she is about our relationship. She always told me that, and I always have to remind her that my mom had me at fifteen and Michael at seventeen. We all grew up together and losing Michael was the biggest challenge we've ever faced. Courtney says, "Still, she's understanding. More than my mom will ever be." I only take a sip of my drink. I don't ask her what she means.

I listen to Courtney talk, and it feels nice to finally speak to her again. It's been months, and I don't want to miss out on the changes in her life, if only for one night.

She's in the middle of telling me about the clubs she's joined when my eyes fall back to the park's entrance. It's been at least thirty minutes since I've seen anyone walk past. It's getting late and Germantown is pretty residential. Everyone is either home or in the city for the night.

So it's strange when I see a lone figure, a man, who is both long and gangly, pass by. I recognize him from earlier. His goalie mask is still in place. He's bathed in the shadows of the street. He moves in slow motion, his arms swinging as he walks down the street.

I load the camera and hear Courtney chirp, "Oh, you want to take my picture?"

It breaks me from my focus, but I play it off. "Sure. Move a little this way." I position her so that I can still get the man walking in the background.

Not a moment later, someone else passes by the park's entrance. It's the *Friday the 13th* kid. He's wearing the same charred mask and stained blue jumpsuit. But something is off about him. He looks taller now. His shoulders are broader. But it's him. I know it is. I wish I could develop the picture I took earlier and compare the two.

I take another picture of Courtney with the kid in the background. He doesn't pass the entrance of the park as the man did. He comes inside, and I watch him approach Hugo and his friends. They've run out of toilet paper and are hanging in a circle, talking amongst themselves.

They pause when the kid approaches them, and I hold my breath for some reason.

"Who's that?" Courtney asks casually as she gets another beer.

"I saw him earlier tonight," I say.

I watch their body language as they talk. Hugo and his friends start gravitating closer together, away from the kid. Hugo glances over at us and the goalie mask kid follows his gaze. My palms suddenly feel sweaty. Even though I can't see his face, I know he's staring at me.

Hugo says something and his friends laugh. He puts a hand on the kid's shoulder. Maybe he made a joke at his expense, and the pat on the shoulder is a way to tell him to lighten up... but the kid freezes. He looks at Hugo's hand on his shoulder, and it happens so fast. He grips his wrist and snaps his hand back.

"Shit!" Courtney yells. She stands to her feet, but I hold her wrist to stop her from going over.

Hugo's friends both step back and I can hear Hugo's cry. "What the fuck? I think you broke my wrist." He's bent on the ground, cradling his arm.

"Hugo," Courtney takes another step, but I stop her. She looks back at me, and I shake my head. "Why don't you want me to go over there?" she asks.

Her question gets answered a second later when the kid unbuttons the top of his jumpsuit and pulls out a long, serrated knife. It's wet and gleams under the moonlight. The kid takes a step forward and Hugo falls back to the ground. His friends take off.

"What the hell?" Courtney whispers, but then she cups her hands. "Run, you idiot!"

The kid turns his head slowly and faces us.

I grab Courtney's hand and we move.

My hat flies off my head as I run, and I let go of Courtney's hand to catch it. And I want to catch it because it used to be Michael's, but fumbling for even a second makes me realize that he has others at home.

Courtney is right on my heels and once we run out of the park together, we keep going.

I glance back before the park is out of view and see the kid, walking at a normal pace towards us. His knife is at his side, dripping onto the ground as he moves. Once we step off the sidewalk into the street, Courtney's kitten heels clack against the asphalt. I slow down when I realize she's straggling behind me.

"Take the damn shoes off!"

"Damn it!" she yells. She kicks the shoes off, and they fly in the street. We book it now, staying close together, breathing heavily, legs burning. We turn onto Tulpehocken. The street is silent. Orange street lamps dot the sidewalk.

We stumble to a stop in the middle of the street when we see movement. A figure, long,... impossibly tall... emerges from the shadows. There's one, then another. They move slowly from the shadows of the trees. They both face us, standing under the orange streetlamp. They also wear charred, broken goalie masks and blue stained jumpsuits.

I suddenly feel Courtney's hand grip my fingers. Her mouth hangs open, looking behind us. Down Tulpehocken, another figure is there, a silhouette outlined in the shadows.

Courtney's grip tightens in my hand and we move again. We go down Greene Street instead. The side street is covered in darkness except for a few slivers of moonlight filtering through the large trees. We run fast enough to gain distance between them and us. I stop when I see a space between two parked cars.

We duck there, laying flat on the gravel. Courtney's body shakes beside me. When she shudders, I see that she's crying. It's weird. I don't know what's happening, but somewhere in my mind, I know it's still Halloween. I know this must be a prank. But the fear is real.

Finally stopping, and feeling my body trying to catch its breath, I notice Courtney isn't the only one shaking.

I don't know the plan, but my house is too far away to keep running through the neighborhood like this. I glance across the street at a house decorated with pumpkins and bats hanging on their porch. There's a light on in their front room. Maybe they'll let us use their phone.

I'm about to tell Courtney my plan when something moves in the corner of my eye.

Across the street, there's a dark shadow between two parked cars. I can see the top of a head. I try to get a better look and I remember Hugo suddenly, and his friends. I didn't see where they ran off to. They could still be at the park, or maybe they ran home. Or maybe this is one of them, having the same idea as me to hide.

The shadow moves and white, long fingers claw out from the darkness, raking the street with its nails.

Courtney's grip nearly breaks my hand.

The head of the silhouette emerges and under the moonlight, I see the beginning of a goalie mask. The figure breaks from his hiding spot, standing up between the cars, but... he goes on for too long. He's unfolding, getting taller and taller, still in the process of standing to his full height, but never quite getting there.

He finally stops when his head touches the lowest branch of a tree. I see his blue jumpsuit, long arms, and thin, white hands. He takes a step out from between the cars and his legs move awkwardly, like he's not used to moving them. He's a lot

136

taller than the other ones we've seen. I can't make out his face from the ground, and I don't want to. I don't want to see it.

Courtney makes a muffled sound, and he snaps his head in our direction. Courtney squints her eyes shut and covers her mouth with her hand. He moves slowly towards us. I don't know if we should run or pretend we aren't here. Courtney shuffles closer to me, and I feel something hard and round press into my leg.

I realize it's the jawbreaker Lori gave me earlier. My hand snakes into my pocket, and I curse in my mind because I have *so much shit* in there. The camera, Lori's flashlight, my house keys, until I finally grab the jawbreaker.

I don't think it through. I don't plan anything out. I pull the jawbreaker from my pocket and roll it down the street.

He turns quickly and races towards the sound. His long arms and legs clamber after the jawbreaker, and his body moves like a giant spider. The image makes my knees feel like jelly. While his back is turned, I help Courtney to her feet. We quickly, and quietly, head in the opposite direction. We run until we reach Germantown Avenue where there are many lights and cars passing by.

It's a sense of relief to be around life again. I glance back and don't see anything there. No tall men with long legs. No sign of a kid with a goalie mask wielding a knife.

I tell Courtney to follow me, and we hurry to my house, ensuring we stay in the light and take the busiest streets to get there.

Mom is genuinely confused to see us at the front door and even more when she sees Courtney's bare feet. I tell her some kids played a trick on us tonight, and we had to get home. Mom insists on Courtney staying for the night and when she goes upstairs, Courtney finally speaks.

"You think it was just a trick?"

"I mean, they were dressed like Jason-"

"They were *tall*, like freakishly tall. And that thing between the cars?"

The memories play back in my mind, and a cold shiver snakes up my spine. "I don't know."

"I hope Hugo got home safe. I'll call him in the morning." Courtney relaxes on the couch. She pouts when she looks at her feet. "I loved those shoes."

I get her some blankets for her to sleep on the couch. When I move to go up to my room, she holds onto my arm. "Can you sleep down here? With me?"

I look at her curled on the couch. Her braids have fallen from her ponytail. She has a few smudges on her face, probably from lying under the cars. I wonder if I look like hell, too.

"Okay," I say, but she stops me when I try to lay in the recliner. She pulls me on top of her, and we lay together. She fans the blanket around us and holds me.

"Thank you for helping me get away, Mal," she whispers into my hair. "I didn't deserve that, after what happened between us." I don't say anything, but she squeezes me. "Tonight was so effin' scary. Holy shit. I don't think I'll ever see

Halloween the same. Good thing it was all just some prank, right?" she says.

I think about the goalie mask kid... the way he laughed when I first saw him. And the tall men... and the extremely tall one from between the cars. Using stilts is the only logical explanation for their impossible height. But then how did that one bend so low between the cars? How the hell did they pull that off? And why? Just to scare us?

I fall asleep that night, lying on top of Courtney, telling myself, it's just a trick. It was all a trick.

—

The next day, Mom waits until Courtney has left and we're alone to tell me that some kids went missing last night. Apparently they'd gone trick-or-treating, but they never made it home. The goalie mask kid has never left my mind. His knife had blood on it, I'm sure. But no... it was only a prank. It wasn't real.

I call Courtney later that night, only to check on her. I'm not sure if our relationship is back to how we were before, but I have to see the aftermath of last night through. She seems actually relieved to hear from me. She tells me that Hugo got away and that freaky kid had actually broken his wrist. Hugo said he'd kill him if he ever saw him again. I ask about his friends and Courtney goes silent. She says one of them is missing. He didn't come home.

The next time I come back home is for Thanksgiving break, and the events from Halloween night become a distant nightmare. I try to forget about it, and I do. It's not until one night after dinner when I'm sitting with my mom on the couch that I realize that night was far from over for me.

Mom asks about my photography and mentions she had the film developed from Halloween night, but she hasn't had a chance to look through them yet. Curiosity pulls me violently and I ask to see them.

She tells me they're in the junk drawer in the kitchen. I don't want to seem too eager, and also I'm a little afraid of what I may see, so I wait until later that night.

After Mom goes upstairs for bed, I go to the kitchen and find the pictures. I break the seal on the envelope. I set the small stack of photos on the counter. The first picture is of Lori and Laura in their fairy princess costumes, posing in front of our house. But behind them... my mouth drops.

I flip to the next one. There it is again.

I go on to the next one, flipping through photo after photo. My skin breaks into goosebumps with each one I see. This can't be right. I even check the negatives, and it's there. *He's* there. In every picture I took that night, the kid... the one with the goalie mask is there, like a ghost in the background.

I take out the last two pictures of the stack, which I took of Courtney at the park. The first one is of the tall man walking in the background. I remember him walking slowly, but in this picture, he's a blur, as if he'd been running. "The hell?"

Then I look at the last photo. Courtney is there, smiling wide. Her brown eyes are marred by red-eye, but in the back is the kid again, walking into the park like I remembered. But... something is off about this. I don't remember his goalie mask being off. I don't remember him looking at us when he walked in, but here, he's looking right at the camera. He's even waving, like he purposely posed for the picture.

And without his mask, I can finally see his face. I peer further into the photo, and my blood runs cold when I see his smile. I drop the photo on the counter like it's on fire. My heart hammers in my chest as I gaze around the kitchen. I'm afraid to look at the photo again, but I know I need to look again. I have to be sure.

I pick up the photo. I'm not mistaken. The kid in the goalie mask, smiling brightly at the camera... is my brother. It's fucking Michael.

viii. william

They call me Fresh. Like *The Fresh Prince.* We were both born and raised in West Philadelphia until my family moved to Germantown. And like the Fresh Prince, we're both named Will. We both like making people laugh. I have a faded hightop like he did as a teen, but that's... unrelated. And I guess that's where our similarities end.

One thing about me is I don't let anyone try to play me. It doesn't happen much because I can joke back. But when it's Tariq, for some reason, I always choke.

Like now, as we sit at the back of the class, I know he's looking at my mp3 player. I ignore him until I hear him chuckle. "What, man?" I ask.

"Nothing." Tariq raises his hands in surrender. He sits across from me in class. "What are you listening to?"

"Beanie Sigel," I say. He nods with a smirk, and I roll my eyes. "What?"

"*Man,* that dusty ass mp3." He waves and our friends laugh. "You don't have an iPod?"

My mp3 isn't the newest, but it's not old. It's a little chipped around the edges and has a small crack on the screen. Now that I think about it, I don't really remember how I got it.

"Who you callin' dusty?" I say with a smile. "With your broke-ass sneakers." Our friends laugh. "Them jawns not even *real* Jordans! Ol' Canal Street lookin' ass."

Tariq laughs and shakes his head. "All right, all right." He brushes nonexistent dirt from the side of his sneakers.

"Boys, come on," our teacher calls from the front of the classroom. "If you don't pay attention, you won't last very long."

I blink. "What?"

She sighs and puts her hand on her hip. "If you don't pay attention, you won't pass the test on Friday." She goes back to teaching the front half of the room.

"If she don't shut up, man," Tariq says, and a few people laugh.

143

I turn to say something to him when the overhead speaker turns on. It crackles until Principal Jenkins greets the school. "Good morning Germantown High!" she calls loudly.

"I know that news of the school's closing can be a downer, but we will always be Germantown High proud in our hearts. As we finish the school year's end and say farewell to our graduating class of 2013, I'm happy that we're going off with a bang. A big, big congratulations to the Bear's football team with a 38-15 win!" A big round of cheers sounds from the classroom and outside in the hall. "If you see our team, make sure you give them a big-"

The loudspeaker cuts out. It doesn't crackle, like hearing a landline phone hang up. No, it just... turns off.

I look at Tariq, and he's sitting in his seat, looking straight ahead. So are our friends Keshawn, Mike, Lodi, and Juke. My teacher stands at the front of the class, her hand on the white-erase board. Her back is turned towards us, but her hand isn't moving. She isn't writing.

The entire class is frozen, like someone has pressed pause. And it's quiet. So quiet.

A scream rips through the hallway, echoing until it reaches the classroom. "God, please! Someone help me!"

My heart thumps, and I stand out of my seat, but I see something out of the corner of my eye. Tariq. He isn't looking at me, but he shakes his head. Slowly.

I sit back down and become still, staring ahead like everyone else. The screams don't stop. They become louder, drawing nearer until I can hear sneakers running up the linoleum floor. Their breathing is heavier.

Then I see him. He isn't really fast, stumbling over himself when he passes by the doorway. It's one of the football players, wearing the team's green jacket, but something is different about this one. There's blood covering the entire front. When he turns around, I see why he's stumbling around.

His eyes have been gouged out.

"Please," he cries as he shuffles forward, his arms out in front. "Someone help me... help me..."

His voice dies out as he gets further away, and I try everything within me not to move. To not cry out. To not throw up. I glance around the room without turning my head and no one has moved an inch. Miss Perry is still frozen. My class is still frozen. And the clock above the doorway... that's frozen, too.

I'm about to move when I hear a soft clicking sound. Equal in measure. I hold my breath and wait, listening as it gets closer. It's coming from the hallway, coming down in soft clicks and I count.

Click. One, two, three. *Click.* One, two, three.

It sounds outside the doorway, and I grip the side of my desk when I see it. A figure with a hooded red cloak. Its face is hidden, but it has a lumpy hunched back and horns twisting from underneath the hood. It moves slowly across the doorway, holding a wooden staff. The staff hits the ground as it glides forward.

Click. One, two, three. *Click.* One, two, three.

And then it's gone.

I release a breath and a second later, class starts again.

Our teacher finishes writing out the formulas on the board. Conversation starts again and on the loudspeaker, Principal Jenkins finishes her announcement. "...high five! Go Bears!"

"Go Bears!" the class responds.

"What the hell?" I look at Tariq, and he's staring at his empty notebook, rubbing his lip in thought. He looks over at me, but says nothing.

When I open my mouth, he shakes his head. "Don't."

Once the bell rings, Tariq is the first to leave. I want to grip him by the arm and ask him questions, but if he's willing to act like nothing happened, then that's him. I'm getting the hell out of here.

It's possible that I dreamt the entire thing. Sometimes I sleep during pre-Calculus. But no, it felt too real. I would've remembered falling asleep. I would *know* that I was dreaming. And *that shit* was not a dream.

I hurry past other students in the hallway, making my way to the first floor, but as I get closer to the steps, the hallways get more and more crowded.

A kid steps on my foot, and I push him back. It's someone from my English class and he looks at me with fear in his eyes. "Sorry, Fresh," he says, and then he's lost in the sea of students.

I keep trying to pass. The lockers seem to stretch on in this hallway forever. More kids surround me, trying to get to their classes. Someone bumps into me hard, and I fall back onto the ground. "Yo, what the fuck?"

No one notices me on the floor. Where did all these kids come from? The school only houses juniors and seniors *and* a lot of the students have left for charter schools. It shouldn't be this packed.

I try to get up, but get knocked back down. It keeps happening. Over and over until I'm holding my head on the floor, trying not to get my head trampled.

—

I'm in the cafe, sitting next to Tariq. The table shakes in front of me and when I look up, I see why. Lunch trays are in front of us, but they sit to the side. Juke is at the end of the table with that big smile, banging on the table while everyone else follows the beat.

Suddenly my ears pop, and I can finally hear again. The sound of the loud cafeteria is overwhelming, and I cover my ears until I can adjust. Tariq is still beside me, freestyling to Juke's beat. His turn finishes a second later, and I nudge him while Mike takes his turn.

"Riq, what is this?"

Tariq stares ahead, a smile on his face, still banging on the table. "Come on, man. It's almost your turn."

"I don't care about this." I stand from the table, and Tariq stops. Our friends continue without us, so I pull him closer. "What *the hell* just happened?"

He shrugs his shoulders. "I don't know, man-"

"Come on, son." I push on an impulse, but he doesn't shove me back. "There's some crazy shit goin on. I saw a kid without eyes. There's some... some like monster-"

"Whoa, Fresh." Tariq raises his hands. He even smiles, making me want to smack the shit out of him. "You're tweakin', man. I don't know what you're talking about." He tilts his head towards the table. "Come on, play along." He doesn't wait for me and returns to the table, banging on it without missing a beat.

I take a deep breath and scan the cafe. It's filled with students, talking and laughing and I'm just standing here, trying not to scream to the fucking ceiling.

Then I see Jalissa. She's sitting by herself beneath a banner congratulating the upcoming graduating class of 2013. Her shirt is the same color blue as the banner. It's a weird thing to notice as I walk up to her.

She lifts her head as I approach. God, she's so pretty. I almost forget about this nightmare when she looks at me. Her hair is slicked back into a low puff and my eye catches the gleam from her chain necklace sitting on her chest.

"Fresh." She grins. "Where you been at?"

"Lis, hey." I sit across from her. "Look, there's something weird going on."

Her brows cinch together. "What do you mean?"

"I mean, I'm seeing some really crazy shit. And I tried to leave school, but..." I don't know how to explain it to her. "I mean there's something off. I don't even remember coming to

148

school today. Everyone is acting weird. Even Riq. And the shit…" I rub my face with my hands. "I'm losing my mind-"

"Okay, okay." She touches my arm, and I feel myself instantly calm down. "Maybe you should go home."

"I tried!" I yell, and she flinches. "I'm sorry. I'm sorry." I pat her hand. "I tried leaving," I explain calmly. "But again, something weird… I don't know what happened."

Jalissa tilts her head and sighs. She rubs my arm. "I don't know, Fresh, maybe you should-"

She freezes. Her mouth is still posed, her eyes still fixed on me. When I move my head, her eyes don't follow. And then I realize how silent the cafe is. I glance back at Tariq's table and he's there, hand balled into a fist and lifted high, waiting to bang on the table.

"Oh, what the fuck."

I try to move, but Jalissa's hand is still on my arm. Her fingers won't move, even when I try to jerk myself free.

Then in the quiet, I hear it again. The scream.

"Is someone there?" The voice echoes through the cafe and sends chills up my spine. "Please, someone."

A kid enters the cafe. It's the kid from my English class. The one who stepped on my foot in the hallway. My stomach flips.

Blood runs down his cheeks from his empty eye sockets. He walks, arms outstretched, bumping into tables. "Someone, help me, please. He's coming."

"Shit." I pull even harder from Jalissa's grip. It's loosening, but not fast enough. "Fuck, come on." I'm pulling harder. Faster. And the kid is shuffling closer.

"I hear someone there, please!"

My arm finally comes free, and I fall out of my seat. The kid is shuffling forward, and I hide underneath the table. I don't mean to be fresh and cling onto Jalissa's legs, but it's the only thing that makes me feel safe.

I watch the kid, from his waist down, as he bumps into my table. His hands smack the surface. "Are you there? Please, help me... Please..."

I cover my mouth and clench my eyes shut. I wish I could cover my ears, but I can't. I'm forced to hear this kid beg for my help. I'm forced to hear the sudden click of a staff as it enters the cafe.

"He's coming! No! Please!" He bangs the table one more time before shuffling away.

The soft click comes closer. Three seconds between each time the staff hits the floor. I can't see where it's at, but by the sound of it, it's coming from the other side of the cafe.

A sudden flash of dark red appears by my table. My grip tightens on Jalissa's legs. Long gray feet poke from out of its long robe. Its toes are long and ashy. Gnarly yellow nails almost touch my shoes.

I clench my eyes shut again. I can hear it breathing, heavy and loud. And then it sniffs. Like a long, deep inhale before releasing a groan. My heart falls to my stomach. I watch as it slowly lifts the cane and bangs it on the floor.

—

"...and then when you complete that section, move onto Chapter 5."

I immediately rise from my desk. Papers and my science textbook are in front of me. "What the hell?" I shout.

"Mr. William Hawkins." My science teacher removes the glasses from her face. "I don't like outbursts and I *don't* like swearing. Now, sit down."

I do as she says, and my class chuckles as she finishes her instructions. Everyone is laughing, except Tariq.

"Now, break into your partners." She dismisses us, and I hop over to Tariq.

I speak low. "You need to answer me, now-"

"Play along," Tariq says. He opens his textbook and starts writing in his notebook. "Play along and don't move."

I scan his face and then glance over the classroom. Everyone else is busy at work. "I don't understand. Why can't I leave?"

"You saw what happened," Tariq says casually as he turns the page. "He won't let us."

"Who is he?"

"I don't know." He doesn't look at me. He keeps his head down, writing profusely. When I look at the notes, I see that he isn't even writing from the textbook. It's just full of random words. "But if you play along and stay still, he'll leave you alone."

"How do you know this?"

"I woke up like you did, just a few days ago," he says. He stops writing and looks at me. "We've been doing this day over and over-"

"Riq, come on."

"I'm serious," he says. Tariq and I are like brothers. So when he looks at me like this, with... fear in his eyes, I have to believe him. "I've seen some shit, Fresh."

"And I haven't?"

"Just, please. Play along."

"*No,*" I draw the word out slowly. "We are getting out of here. The fuck you mean?"

"I don't think that's-"

The room suddenly grows quiet. I roll my head back. "You have *got* to be kidding me."

Tariq rolls into position immediately. He freezes, his hand is positioned over his notebook like he's about to write another word.

I sit still at the desk beside him and stare straight ahead. Our class is frozen, our teacher is bent over, helping a pair of partners and her hand is frozen on her glasses like she just put them back on her face.

I wait to hear the screams. I wait to hear a poor kid who's been battered and bloodied and hopelessly searching the hallways for help, but never finds it. Instead, I hear the click. It's closer this time.

Click. One, two. *Click.* One, two.

My heart is beating faster and I want to look over at Tariq, but I can't without turning my head. The staff is moving even faster.

Click. One. *Click.* One.

Click. Click. Click. Click.

It stops.

My eyes stare straight ahead, my gaze is unwavering.

The hooded figure appears at the doorway, and the staff clicks when it steps inside the classroom. I hold my breath and I'm struggling to keep my eyes open. Don't blink. Don't blink. Don't...

Tariq speaks one simple word. Softly, under his breath. The hooded figure is staring right at him. Its hood still masks its face in darkness, but there's no doubt about it. It's staring at Tariq.

"Shit," is all he says and the hooded figure moves in a flash of red.

I stare ahead, gripping the side of my desk as I hear Tariq scream. I hear a crunch and a growl so deep, so unlike anything that I've ever heard in my life. Then squelching and warm liquid squirts on my pant legs. It splashes on the side of my face, but I still don't move. I don't think I can.

And just a moment later, the figure straightens up, takes his staff and glides out of the classroom.

Click. One, two, three. *Click.* One, two, three.

Sound suddenly floods my ears. Students go back to talking, pages turning in a textbook, and the teacher gives help to a pair of partners.

My lip trembles. They carry on, but I'm still frozen. I can't get up. I can't even move. The teacher stands before me.

"Mr. Hawkins, I don't think you have a partner today. Why don't you join..." her voice continues, but I drown her out. I finally turn my head and take in the sight beside me.

Tariq's desk is covered in blood and he's still there. His head is slumped back. His finger twitches on the desk, his mouth open as blood trickles from his lips. He's still breathing, barely, taking shallow breaths. And like everyone else, his eyes aren't... they aren't...

I lean over and vomit on the floor and our teacher barely bats an eye. She only steps back and points to the side of my face. "You have something on your face." I touch my cheek and when I gaze at my fingers, dabs of blood stain the tips. "Maybe you should go clean up-"

I struggle to my feet and push past her. My knees and entire lower body are so weak that I lean on every desk until I leave the classroom. "I gotta get... out." My voice feels dry.

The hallways are empty and silent. I pass the lockers, I pass the Malcolm X mural, getting more comfortable on my feet until I'm jogging. The first floor isn't far, but when I turn to where the stairwell is, I'm somewhere completely different.

I'm in the hallway that leads to the closed-off wing of the high school. Windows line the left side until it disappears into the darkness at the end of the hall. Construction tape is covered over where the lights are turned off.

Standing before it, facing the darkness, is a girl in a blue shirt and a low puff.

"Jalissa," I call out. I run to her. "Come on. We gotta go."

"Fresh?" Her voice is fragile, like she's on the verge of tears. "Please, help..." She turns around.

"Shit!" I slip, falling right on my back. "No, Lis... no."

Her hands try to find me. She takes small steps forward. "Help me, Fresh."

I gaze at her beautiful face, now marred and bloodied. Her brown eyes are now gone, replaced with gory darkness.

It suddenly gets darker. The hallway lights turn off and are replaced with moonlight coming through the broken and shattered windows. Across the street is the First United Methodist Church and cars drive by on the side street.

I go up to the window. I see a guy in a hoodie walking his dog. I wave my arms so he'll look up and see me. "Help! Please, help us!" He should hear me. The cold wind flows in from the broken windows. "Please!"

The words die in my mouth when I feel someone step behind me. Looming, towering over my head. The staff clicks just once as it stands still.

"Fresh, I think," Jalissa whispers. "I think he's here."

My reflexes hit and I swing behind me. I miss. But it doesn't matter, because I'm already running. Running past him, running away from Jalissa, running blindly through the darkness.

I nearly slip on random papers and banners on the ground. Lockers are opened and abandoned. And I pass it all until I find the stairs that lead to the first floor. Finally.

I go down one flight, slip on someone's discarded bookbag, and slam into the wall. I stand on my feet in a second and turn to go down the second flight of steps, but then I freeze where I stand.

The steps, the entire hallway leading to the front of the school is flooded with people. They're walking aimlessly, moaning, crying out, pleading for help. Blood runs from their empty eyes.

My hand covers my mouth, but I scream anyway. My hand trembles down the banister as I take in the sight. I scan the floor, looking for a way out.

But when I step off the last step, someone blocks me.

It's Tariq. His head tilts to the ceiling like he's listening for me. I can't look into his face, not without falling apart.

He grips my shoulders. "Fresh, I'm sorry. I thought playing along would help-"

"It's okay." My head is still facing the floor. "We can still make it out. We can-"

"We can't. We can't open the doors. He won't let us." His bloody hands tighten their grip on my shoulders. "He already knew who he wanted. Everyone is in order. Jalissa... me..." He turns me around and on the top of the steps is the creature, standing still. "And now it's you."

The creature removes his dark red hood and its head is covered with eyes. Bloody and dark and shifting back and forth.

"I'm sorry, Fresh."

—

I can't see. My hand traces the wall as I shuffle from locker to locker. My throat is raw from screaming, but I still try to speak. "Please..." I whimper. "Please, someone, anyone help me. Please."

Oct. 21, 2019

I'd be the first person to say that the supernatural is a falsehood; a misrepresentation of things that science can and has explained. Throughout history are examples of people misinterpreting natural phenomena as the supernatural. In some respects, it's an idea meant to persuade us that there are far worse things out there than what humans do to each other everyday. Many people have lived in fear, not speaking their truth, and lived unable to be authentically themselves for fear of karma. Or hell.

Some people are more middle of the road. For instance, people like my sister, Jolene, give themselves an out. They don't outwardly believe in the supernatural but give it space to exist.

Some years ago, while retelling an old unexplainable childhood story, Jolene raised her arms in a "don't shoot the messenger" sort of way and declared, "Hey Nate, you never know. Could be true. Could be a lie. One thing's for certain. I don't need anyone or *anything* out there trying to make me a believer."

That always stuck with me. Jolene was a lawyer and by all accounts, a logical, Type A person. She never saw any sort of evidence of the supernatural, yet she'd never deny the possibility of its existence, just in case.

In case of what? I didn't think there was anyone or anything out there preying on non-believers of the supernatural. Jolene would say that I shouldn't speak on things I didn't know about, but when this topic would arise, I'd always assure her I wasn't concerned. But I'm writing this passage to recount recent situations I just cannot explain.

The air had a revitalizing crispness to it. Autumn in my home state of Pennsylvania was one of my favorite times. I know I'm not alone in feeling this way. I once read that most people in the U.S. claim Fall as their favorite season. The leaves are changing, the summer weather fades to cool, and festivals and apple picking abound.

Participating in every bar crawl Germantown and surrounding neighborhoods had to offer was very high on my list. They were great for meeting with friends, relaxing, and enjoying great brews. Last week, I decided on a bar crawl that was occurring on Saturday. I got off work on Friday, did some grocery shopping, and phoned Jolene to see if she'd like to join. She declined. Apparently, things with her boyfriend were getting serious. He was flying her out of the country as a surprise for the next week or so.

I couldn't help but feel slightly annoyed at this, but deep down I was happy for my older sister. She truly deserved every ounce of happiness she could squeeze from this life.

Resolved to leave for the bar crawl alone, I made arrangements to meet some friends. I wasn't the least bit surprised to see only one made it. Entering the first bar, my eyes scanned the crowd. It was a decent turnout. I saw my coworker,

Eileen, sitting on a bar stool, her knapsack holding a space for me to sit down. She smiled warmly, and we began drinking.

As the night wore on, I could tell Eileen was losing steam. It was half past 11, and she kept yawning. Taking her cue, I hailed a car for her to get home safely. She didn't put up a fight. We stood with many others outside a pub on Germantown Avenue, chatting and waiting for our rides.

It was somewhat warm that night, and a dense fog blanketed the cobblestone street. When her car arrived, I ensured the license plate matched and helped Eileen into the car. She nearly tripped over the old trolley tracks as she entered the backseat of her car, but I caught her. I closed her door and waved goodbye. When I stepped back onto the sidewalk, only a few people were left.

As minutes wore on, the pool of people dwindled to just two. Me and a woman who looked to be my age, rocking a bald head and huge gold hoop earrings. She had on minimal makeup and was downright gorgeous.

Her ride soon came. She paused before getting inside and looked back at me.

"You've been waiting a while. Do you want to ride with me?"

I gently waved her off. "Oh no, thank you. I'm okay waiting."

She stood still, her eyes locked on mine. "Are you absolutely sure?" She didn't blink, and although she was a pretty girl, it was unnerving. I nodded. She shook her head as she got into the backseat and drove off. She looked at me one last time through the glass as she rode by.

It felt quiet. The bar was closed, and I was sure the staff had gone home already. Down the block, businesses were closed, too, or locking up for the night. No cars were driving past, which I found to be a bit odd.

I needed to use the bathroom. I checked the car's status and saw it was seven minutes away. My bladder could wait.

I was tempted to call Jolene to see if her plane landed, but I decided against it. I didn't want to disrupt her time away. My back leaned against the bar's window and I watched the traffic lights at the corner change. Red. Green. Yellow. Red. Green. Yellow.

A moment later I saw the illumination of a large yellow light making its way through the fog. It drove right through the red light. I peered into the fog, trying to make out the slow-moving vehicle until I saw the "23" on a long rectangular sign.

It was an old school trolley, split between two colors: green and white. I pressed my back further against the bar's glass window as I dug into my pocket for my phone. I quickly snapped a photo.

The trolley rolled to a stop about a quarter block away.

The doors opened and a man, garbed in a long black trench coat, stepped out. He stood still for a moment before stepping up on the curb and walking up the block.

My breath caught in my throat. My hand found the door handle of the pub and tried giving a push. Of course, it was still locked.

The man stopped in front of a Little Free Library stand and stuck something inside. He walked back to the trolley and boarded. The trolley slowly rolled backward, disappearing into the fog it came from.

Before I could think, my legs led me to the little box of books. Through the glass, there was only one book inside.

"The Strange Accounts of Germantown and Other Peculiar Phenomena..."

It intrigued me enough so I grabbed it and jogged back to the bar as a black Camry pulled up. My phone beeped letting me know that my driver was here. I got inside without looking back.

"Hey," I started. I tried for minutes thinking of a way to ask my question without sounding absurd, "Did you drive down Germantown Ave to get here?" The driver nodded.

"Did you happen to see the trolley?" Our eyes met in the rearview mirror and he chuckled.

"The trolley stopped running over 20 years ago." He shook his head. "I think you've had a few too many."

I flipped through the book and saw eight chapters in the table of contents. I turned the book over. There was no author. Just some sort of riddle on the back cover and the inside page.

I started reading the first story. Something about a man seeing a creepy horse and carriage on Germantown Avenue. I finished it just as the driver pulled up to my apartment.

Oct 22, 2019

I talked to Jolene today. I sent her the trolley photo since she didn't believe me.

"Did you get it?"

"This is fake," she said with little conviction.

"Jolene, I swear it's not."

She sighed deeply and went silent. "That's really weird, Nate. I even made it bigger to see the details, not that I'm an expert. But yeah, it's weird. It's really weird."

"The trolley stopped in front of one of those Little Libraries. You know the ones where you leave a book or borrow one?"

"Mmhm," she mumbled.

"Well," I continued. "This man got off, put a book in, then got back on the trolley. The whole thing just drove off into the fog. Completely disappeared. I looked to see what he dropped off, and it was a book. A weird little thing about creepy stories in Germantown. No author, though."

"Germantown? That's... creepy, Nate."

"Yeah. I read one of the stories. It's definitely up your alley. I can give it to you once you get home from your trip."

We spent another ten minutes talking about what she believed Ryan's plans were regarding their life together. I figured he might propose while they were in Hawaii. I mean, who wouldn't? It's a beautiful place.

Oct 23, 2019

I walked my labrador, Lola, tonight. I always took the same route. I walked down Germantown Avenue, took a few side streets, went down Bayton, and past the old high school. I normally go to bed pretty late, so I consistently take Lola for a walk around ten every night. She loved late night walks. The air was chilly, so I slipped on a gray hoodie just in case we opted for a longer walk.

We made our way down Germantown Avenue. All was quiet except the occasional sound of a car passing by. We got to the corner of Tulpehocken, and I heard something strange as we waited for the light to change.

It sounded like horse hooves clomping against the cobblestone street.

I glanced left then right, fear plunking into my stomach like a stone. I searched for the source of the sound, but the street was empty. It sounded like it was getting closer. Lola whimpered and tugged at her leash. Horses whinnied in the distance.

Lola and I crossed the street to head home. The clomping started to fade, the further we got away from the corner. I looked over my shoulder as we walked; the street wasn't empty like before. A couple casually crossed the adjacent street. A young girl stood on the corner, waiting for the bus, her face illuminated by the glow of her phone screen.

I took a deep breath and hurried to get home.

By the time I got to my apartment, I was paranoid that someone had followed me back. I double padlocked the door and opened a can of beer. I relaxed on my couch and scrolled through Netflix. I chose a nature show, but my mind kept going back to that strange book. My curiosity won over, and I picked it up again.

Starting from the beginning, I began to read. I didn't finish the last story until 3:20 in the morning. My nerves were jumbled, and I wasn't sure if it was from what I'd just read or from being extremely tired.

I climbed into bed and turned off the lamp. That night, just to lighten my mood, I slept to the sounds of old cartoons playing on my TV.

Oct 25, 2019

I called off work yesterday. I wasn't feeling well. I'm still not.

Things have been very... strange lately and I can't explain it. I've never experienced hallucinations, but I think these come pretty close.

In the last two days, I've witnessed things I've never seen, heard, or *smelled* before. And when I look around, no one else is ever aware of it.

Yesterday was a cool Autumn day. Leaves were falling and covering the streets, making them especially hazardous. I needed to go downtown, so I took the bus. I waited at the stop and ducked under the shelter due to the drizzling rain.

Across the street, an all-black Bentley pulled up to the sidewalk. It was a nice car, so naturally, I watched to see who was driving it.

The car door opened, and a Black man stepped out. He wore dark clothes, tailored finely. He took out an umbrella and opened it over his head. He must've felt me staring, because he looked over at me. He grinned, and his teeth were impossibly white.

"Cheers, mate." He chuckled.

The bus pulled up to the stop and blocked him from my view. I was a bit dumbfounded. The driver had to yell to get my attention.

I boarded, and the bus pulled off. I paid my fare and sat in the back. My mind was elsewhere as the bus stopped again. People entered and exited the bus in quiet shuffling.

I was on my way to the library downtown to pick up a book about histories of strange phenomena. I couldn't get these stories out of my mind. I needed to research and look deeply into what exactly this book was.

As I scrolled on my phone, looking through information about authorless books, I smelled a hint of something. It wasn't an overwhelmingly strong scent at first, but I definitely knew what it was.

It smelled like soap.

Normally, I would welcome the scent, especially on a public bus surrounded by people, but this was different. The soap smell grew strong, like industrial grade cleaner. Was it the bus seats?

The bus had stilled, letting people off for their stop. I scanned the people sitting in the seats, trying to see if they had a visceral reaction to the scent. But they didn't seem to. They carried on as normal.

The bus doors closed and began to pull off, but not before I looked out the window. I was met with the blue eyes of a man wearing a blue sweater vest with perfectly coiffed blonde hair. He was standing at the bus stop like he'd just gotten off. The rain, coming down even harder now, pelted him all over, but he didn't seem to care.

As the bus pulled away, he grinned, and it felt like I'd licked a 9V battery. My anxiety got even worse when I realized that the soap smell vanished once the man was gone.

I returned home a few hours later with more than enough books about the supernatural, strange phenomena, and authorless books.

I tore into each one. I read the riddle again, breaking it down and trying to decipher what it meant.

The hours wore on, and before I knew it, night had fallen. A lone lamp illuminated my desk while the rest of my apartment was blanketed in darkness. I hadn't eaten dinner again, but I didn't have an appetite.

I called off work for the next day. I felt on edge. I couldn't shake the feeling of eyes watching my every move.

Maybe I was just losing it?

I didn't want to disturb Jolene, but after a few hours looking over the riddle, I caved. I was spiraling. I needed help.

In the wee hours of the morning, Jolene answered on the third call. "What, Nate?" she gruffed. She'd been sleeping.

I gave a brief explanation of my day. The man in black I saw. The man that reeked of soap. I told her about the horses I heard the other night and how it all came to this goddamn book. I felt my voice raising as I explained and Jolene got quieter and quieter. She listened without interrupting, and her concern was palpable.

"Yeah, Nate, um, I actually have a friend who sees a therapist in Germantown. I think you'd benefit from seeing someone soon, like tomorrow morning."

"Okay," I said.

"Why are you speaking so low? You're scaring me, Nate."

I sat up straighter, not realizing I'd been crouching beside my couch the entire time. My head rested against it, and I gazed out the window.

Streetlight from outside poured into my dark apartment and it bathed my windowsill in a soft orange glow.

There, sitting in the open window was a small yellow bird. Its head flitted quickly, hopping and looking around. I watched almost in a trance as it danced.

"Nate?" I couldn't register Jolene's voice. I crawled on my knees towards the window, watching this happy, beautiful bird. I smiled, slightly, when it looked at me.

Suddenly, its neck snapped sharply to the side. It fell off the windowsill to the street below.

I dropped the phone and ran over. Jolene called my name through the speaker.

I opened the window wider and nearly pushed myself out to see the street below me. There was no bird.

My hand slid up my forehead and through my hair. I sank back into the apartment, eyes wide and a chuckle lodged in my throat. I was going crazy.

I got back to the phone, and Jolene was still calling my name. "I'm here, Jo," I said somberly.

"Shit, Nate, you're scaring me. I'm coming home!"

"No!" I shouted. I took a deep breath. "No, Jolene, no. I can handle this. Don't worry about me. Just get me the doctor's name, please?"

Jolene sighed heavily. "Fine. But are you sure? I don't give a damn about this vacation. I'll be on the next flight home."

I reassured her and she returned to the phone moments later.

"Okay, yeah. His name is Dr. Wu. His office is-"

I hung up the phone and let it drop from my fingers. My head fit into my palms and I rubbed my face, a violent cry slowly ripped from within me.

I curled up on the floor with nothing left in me on this early morning.

Oct. 27, 2019

I haven't been to work in about four days, I think. I've lost
track. Jolene keeps calling me. She even sent a friend over
yesterday to my apartment to check on me. I didn't answer. I
stood in the mirror ignoring the incessant buzz of the doorbell,
and instead took in the gaunt face staring back at me. I turned
to the side and saw my ribs beginning to protrude through my
flabby, pale skin. Thinking about the last few days, I couldn't
remember my last meal.

I left the bathroom and eyed the energy drinks surrounding
my laptop like metal sentries.

After Jolene's friend gave up, I sat down and reviewed the
riddle written at the beginning of the book once more. It
taunted me. It was all I thought about.

I knew the answer to escape this hellish nightmare lay
within these stanzas. I finished the entire book twice and things
from these god-awful stories are still haunting me.

This morning I cocooned myself in a thin plaid robe and
took Lola with me to the bodega.

I saw him out of the corner of my eye and around every
corner. The kid with the goalie mask, lazily carrying a knife
coated in crimson blood. He only stood there, but never came
any closer. I was so tired, I ignored him.

I left the store with all the remaining energy drinks they
had. I didn't want to sleep, because the stories found me even
in my dreams.

Lola started to growl as we waited to cross the street. When we could go, I nearly had to drag her to get her to walk. I followed her gaze to see what had her so on edge. It was an advertisement on the side of a bus shelter. The ad was for a Philadelphia accident lawyer, but his face had been vandalized. Someone colored black on his teeth, but his eyes... They were glowing red. Bright, evil, and angry.

They started to fade away seconds later until they disappeared into nothing. I pulled on Lola's leash and got home as quickly as possible.

I was fearful that no matter the amount of energy drinks and research, I couldn't figure out how to escape this nightmare.

In an act of desperation, I grabbed the book, tossed it in the trashcan and set the damn thing on fire. I wanted it out of my life once and for all. I sat back and watched the flames engulf everything in the can.

Before the fire could grow, I doused it and felt some relief. As the smoke cleared, I went into the fridge to grab another energy drink, but when I returned, the book lay in front of my laptop, unharmed.

I stood frozen. Then finally, out of sheer anger, I threw the full energy drink at my TV. The can burst open, spilling down the screen. Lola sat up, her ears perked as she trotted over to me.

I gripped my hair and couldn't fight the tears welling in my eyes. I felt lost and ultimately, that someone or something would be coming for me soon.

I finished the book countless times. Wasn't that what it wanted?

These eight stories ye must conclude.

No, damn the riddle. I'd had enough of these games.

Tonight, I'll jump on the 23 bus to take me back to the Little Library. I'll put the damn thing back where I found it.

This will be someone else's fucking nightmare.

Please don't judge me for this. I need this to be over. I'll get my life back. I won't neglect Lola anymore. I wouldn't worry Jolene anymore. I'll be free from this nightmare.

Oct 28, 2019

The book came back.

Tonight, Lola and I went for our usual walk. I was ready to
go back to our normal routine. Since putting the book back in
the Little Library, I hadn't seen any unexplainable things. I
thought... I thought I was free.

Lola and I passed the abandoned school like we normally
did on our walks. We turned onto Harvey Street and my eyes
flicked to the full moon. It cast white light over the building.
And that's when I heard it. The piercing cry in the dead of
night.

The cry doubled and grew until voices overlapped, and I
could finally hear that they were screaming the same thing in
bone-chilling unison.

"Help us! Please, someone help us!"

Silhouetted against the light of the moon were arms
outstretched from the broken windows, scratched and
bloodied. They cried out, begging for help.

Lola whimpered and bucked until her leash slipped
through my hand. My feet were too frozen to run after her.

I stood there, helplessly confused. I'd given the book back. I
didn't have it. It should've ended.

Above the loud moans and pleas came a voice louder than
them all. He shrieked so loud it pierced my ears.

"Run! Run, he's coming!"

My eyes fell from the top floor of the building, adorned with the flailing arms of the tortured, down to the now wide-open front doors of the dilapidated school.

The moonlight illuminated just a sliver into the entrance, revealing a figure cloaked in dark red. He held a long staff. It clicked as he stepped into the threshold. He slowly reached up and removed his hood. I already knew what it would be and didn't want to see it.

I took off back home, the pleading voices thankfully fading from earshot. When I glanced back, nothing was chasing me, but I couldn't be too certain.

Now, I sit here at my desk, my doors locked and bolted. As I write, I suddenly realize what this book wanted - why I couldn't get rid of it.

Greet a soul with a brotherly kiss.

I tried to write the answer under the riddle on the front, but the book won't let me. Each time I write, the words fade away. So all I can do is write a warning. A plea to anyone who comes across this book to never open it.

Jolene, I hope you never read this, but if you do, and you get to this point, I just want to say I'm so sor

Acknowledgements

We'd like to thank our family who put up with countless conversations about our story prompts and ideas. To our sister, Morgen, who offered the premise for Story #5 (Ebony).

We'd like to thank our editor, Paige Lawson, who got our edits back to us quickly and boosted our confidence with her kind words.

A special thanks to Michelle, our beta reader, who gave us hilarious (and helpful) commentary in real time and took an interest in our stories.

Dominique: I'd like to thank my husband, Anthony, who helped with marketing ideas and kept the baby busy while we brainstormed. Also, thank you to my son, lover of all things spooky. I'd like to thank Khaighnen for taking on the challenge of all the behind the scenes work, who allowed me to just show up with my numerous ideas, and just write.

Kay: I'd like to thank all the kind editors we've talked to and the TikTok community for fanning the flames to push this book out. Also, I'd like to thank my sister, Dominique, for going on this journey with me (chillin' wit me). I appreciate that she spent her valuable time, money, and energy into this passion project. It means the world to me.

About the Authors

Kay Synclaire lives in Philadelphia with her family. She spends her time nannying her niece and nephew, but when she isn't with them, she enjoys reading fantasy books and creating art. She loves listening to movie scores and Kings Kaleidoscope. She's currently working on multiple writing projects and regularly updates on social media through TikTok (@kaysynclaire) and Instagram (@kaysynclairebooks).

Dominique White lives in Philadelphia with her husband and son, and is expecting another child. She's a registered nurse, but when she isn't working, she likes to bake and do arts and crafts. She enjoys listening to 90's RnB and spending time with her family. She occasionally updates her life on social media through TikTok (@discoveringjoy)

Printed in the USA
CPSIA information can be obtained
at www.ICGtesting.com
JSHW060213161023
50208JS00007B/38